WOOLLYB

WOOLLYBACK

ALAN FLEET

an imprint of
ANNE LOADER
PUBLICATIONS

ISBN 1 901253 18 X

First published July 2000
Reprinted December 2000

© Alan Fleet

Published in Gt Britain by:
Léonie Press
an imprint of
Anne Loader Publications
13 Vale Road
Hartford
Northwich
Cheshire CW8 1PL
Tel: 01606 75660   Fax: 01606 77609
E-mail: anne@aloaderpubs.u-net.com
Websites: http://www.aloaderpubs.u-net.com
http://www.leoniepress.co.uk
http://www.sleepydogdreams.com

Typeset and printed by:
Anne Loader Publications

Cover illustration by Patricia Kelsall

About the author

Alan Fleet was born and raised in Winsford. He
has travelled extensively in the international
oil industry, yet apart from three years at
Manchester University, he has lived in
Cheshire all his life.

He devotes much of his time, together with his
family, to the study of Aikido, perhaps the most
spiritual of the martial arts.

Dedication

For my wife Doreen and my children Adam
and Danielle, and also my parents who now
live in the light.
AF

Contents

Chapter 1

My finger gently traces the faint remains of a jagged scar that runs around the base of his thumb. Have I noticed it before? I'm not sure, and even if I have, have I really given it much thought? For that matter, have I really looked at his hands before? No, I haven't, but now I am looking at the man through different eyes, and it's strange how such ordinary observations give way to realisation if you only allow them to. Now as I sit here and look and hold his hand, I wonder. Our hands are so different. Not just because of our ages, but because of what has happened to our hands.

Give myself time to think. It's blindingly obvious why our hands are so different, and it is because he wanted them to be. This man, lying fast asleep and yet not resting, pushed his body manually all his life, his strong hands bearing the legacy of long, hard days, week after week, year after year. My hands are soft, the hands of the educated, the hands he wanted me to have. Through his own aims and goals, though he would never have called them such, he brought about a change in the direction his family would take. But what a change. And when it started did he really want it? And more importantly, could he cope with it? Did he cope with it? How could he? He didn't know what was going to change. He wanted a son like him who was different, a contradiction which neither of us ever came to terms with, and now we have one last night together. Will there be enough time? I squeeze his hand and in his sleep he seems to return the pressure.

I'm not asleep ye know, luv. I'm just not moving. Ye'see, if I keep still I can just about catch enough breath to stop me feeling like I'm suffocating. Just give me a bit longer and I'll sit up and talk. I know why you're staying with me tonight, but I suppose we'll pretend that neither of us knows. It's funny, the night I want to talk more than any other time in my life, I'm just not well enough. Did we talk enough? Don't answer, I already know.

The door opened to the private room. "Mr Harrison," the nurse gently said. I didn't look up. "Mr Harrison," she said again as if prompting me. I looked, she smiled. Odd really, I'm forty years old, but when I'm with my dad he's Mr Harrison and I'm the boy.

"Oh good," she said, looking at my dad, "a short sleep will do him good. I'm just looking in to tell you we change shifts in ten minutes. Are you okay? Do you need a blanket?"

"No thanks. I want to sit up and stay awake in case he wakes."

"Okay," she smiled, "we'll keep looking in through the night."

The door silently closed after her and we were left in the dimly lit room. The birds going to roost in the tree outside the window had finally settled for the night, and everywhere was quiet.

Don't draw the curtains, luv, it's a beautiful sky tonight, full of stars. Let me watch the stars one last time.

I looked at the stars through the large window and decided to leave the curtains open. What a stunning summer night's sky! The stars were so vivid tonight, it seemed a shame to shut them out.

In the peace and tranquillity my mind began to wander again. Changes! Well, we all change through life, everyone knew that, but when you are eleven years old some changes that you have been conditioned to expect have such far-reaching consequences that a busy young boy simply does not have the time or the inclination to appreciate. But be sure he will be confronted by them, and from quarters he could never have imagined. Just like my town of Winsford. Someone had said it should become an overspill town for Liverpool. Winsford had said yes, because it seemed a good idea, and the small town in the middle of the beautiful Cheshire countryside didn't just grow, it exploded. 1964 it was. That year my life and my town changed forever.

Chapter 2

I had woken with a start. Something was on my face. I felt long legs move on my cheeks and a bulbous body was over the side of my nose and left eye. I lay still and breathed slowly as the rubbery legs moved with the gentle intake of each breath. My mind raced as I slowly opened my right eye and saw Sid sitting on my face.

"Stupid spider," I said quietly to myself as my heartbeat began to return to normal. "I've told you to stay on your shelf."

I pulled myself slowly up on my pillow, seeing if I could keep Sid balanced on my face, the elastic tied to Sid's body now hanging over my shoulder.

"Did it! Now back up there."

Sid was returned to the lower shelf, once again purposely balanced on the edge, ready to strike when needed.

Sid was a present from me to me when I went to Chester Zoo the previous year for a birthday treat. Of course, he hadn't always lived on the shelf because they had only been put up just before Christmas by my dad. ("And make sure you keep your room tidy now, or I'll take them down again!"). I was really pleased with the idea of the elastic. It was just long enough for Sid to slip off the shelf, bounce on the bed and then dangle until he finally came to rest two inches off the pillow with all eight legs spread out. He was made of really soft, stretchy, rubbery stuff, with little nobbles all over him. Every time he was touched the whole body and legs seemed to move, almost lifelike. I knew Sid was realistic because my mum had screamed the first time he had slipped off the shelf when she had been making my bed.

I sat there in the darkness facing down my long, narrow bedroom. The strips of light that successfully found their way between the heavy dark curtains produced an effect like something from a science fiction film. Millions of dust particles were bathed in the thin strips of light. I reached under my bed to get some fluff and dust off the lino and then blew it toward the light beams.

"Fantastic!" I coughed, then watched the particles pass through the cleansing L.A.S.E.R. and die. I wished I could remember what L.A.S.E.R. stood for. It was only on the telly two days earlier, and it would have been really flash to say it at school. Just like it had been flash when Mike Hough said the really long name of the Welsh town in front of all the class because his Welsh auntie had taught him. We all thought he was brilliant after that.

"It *will* be today," the old woman's voice said from outside. I bet she's pointing her finger to the floor as well, I thought. If I did that, I'd get told off. I didn't really like Mrs Haspell, she was a bit weird. She lived two doors down at number 3 and always had her back door slightly open. It was impossible to creep past without her spotting you through the crack, and then she would laugh. No, actually it was more of a cackle, but without any joy. There was no malice either, but because she always wore grey and black, and her lights were always off, it was spooky. Daytime was bad enough, but when it was dark it was 'piss yer pants stuff'.

"Oh brilliant!" I said quietly to no-one. "You've thought of the toilet and now you'll 'ave to get up."

Maybe I could hold it, I thought. No chance, I'd have to get up. I got up, but as soon as I stood, the pressure on my bladder was worse. I started to dress quickly, ready for the run down the stairs, through the kitchen, and out across the backyard to the toilet.

"You don't know it'll be today. It's only because of what she said yesterday." Now that was my mum, and she sounded a bit put out by Mrs Haspell.

My underpants and jeans were now on, but I had to look outside to see what was happening. I pulled the curtains back and squinted in the bright daylight.

"Well, she's always been right before." That was Aunty Connie, her voice pleading for friendliness.

"Trust you to stick up for 'er," Mum said.

"She's not sticking up for me. I can stick up for meself, thank you very much. It'll be today." Mrs Haspell folded her arms for good effect. You had to give it to her, she did know how to be irritating.

I flicked the lock across and pulled up the sash window. My mum whirled on her heels at the sound of the window lifting.

"You be careful with that window. Don't lift it too 'igh. You know one of the cords is snapped. It'll jam."

"Good morning, Mother." Too sarcastic.

"Watch it!"

Still, she did smile. She was standing in the backyard, talking over the hedge to Aunty Connie in her backyard, with Mrs Haspell over the hedge in her backyard. All we needed now was Mrs Evans

4

and Mrs Clarke to come out and we would have a full set.

"'Ello Joe."

"'Ello, Aunty Connie."

"Ha, ha, haaaa."

Hello, Mrs Witch would have been good, but I didn't dare with my mum there, so I just grinned back. I pulled my head back inside the window. Blast! Well, I'll have to hold it now because I'm not going to the toilet with those three down there. I put on a clean T-shirt and stuck my head out again.

"Hair!" Mum shouted.

How did she know I'd looked out?

"Ha, ha, haaaa."

Shut up you old witch. I pulled my head back inside. Small comb with thick brown curly hair equals pain. As I struggled to make my hair look neat and tidy the same old conversation seemed to be repeated outside. "Yes she will", "No she won't". Soon it would be time for the crocodile and the sausages to appear.

Once more I stuck my head out of the window, ready for the inspection.

"Better," she said.

Better? This is as good as it gets. I wish I had hair like Tony Curtis in the Vikings. That would be flash.

"I bet you're excited, aren't you?" Aunty Connie asked.

"Course 'e is. Big day for 'im," Mum answered for me.

"You just said I didn't know it was today," the witch said.

"*If* it is today it will be a big day for 'im."

Stop making a fuss, Mum, was what I wanted to say. "I'm fed up with waiting," is what I really said. And then when their backs were turned to look up at me in the window I saw her. She was running up the bank to the cottages. It was in her hand. I'd never seen Jessie the postwoman run before. She'd left her bike at the bottom of our path and was actually running. I knew then that it was good news.

"He's passed! He's passed!" All three turned round like a dance troupe with perfect timing.

"I told you she'd know," the witch said.

"'Ow can she?" Mum asked, frowning.

"Oh, 'ow wonderful, 'e's the first one," Aunty Connie said, beaming.

"If she's opened the letter, she's in for it," mum said, and I knew

5

she meant it. I'd heard that tone before and it meant trouble.

"'E's definitely passed. Look the envelope is white. This year it's white and brown envelopes, last year it was first and second class stamps, the year before it was large and small envelopes. Oh Violet, he's passed. I'm thrilled for you," Jessie managed to gasp out. She really was a bit too big to be running.

My mum's eyes watered as she turned and shouted to me. "You've passed your exams. Are you pleased?" Her face was alight and she hugged the unopened letter to her chest. It meant so much to her and I was glad I made her happy. As for me, passing my exams meant that I was going to the Grammar School, exactly what I wanted. I really didn't know what to say. It was great. I couldn't wait to go and see my mates.

Jessie and Aunty Connie followed my mum inside for a cup of tea, the witch went back to her cauldron and I rushed to the toilet. Within five minutes I'd had a bowl of cornflakes, washed my face, brushed my teeth and was ready for off.

"I'm going for Peter and Mark, to see if they've passed as well." Out of the kitchen I went, into the backyard. Forget about the bike in the shed.

"Joe! Before you go," Mum said from the back door.

"What?" I really was in a rush.

"They might not 'ave passed."

"So?"

"If they 'aven't and they wanted to, they might find it 'ard that you 'ave."

"Nawr, we're friends. See you later." I was running.

"Joe!"

"What?"

"Call at Aunty Joan's and tell 'er."

"No," I shouted, head tilted back and up to the sky. "I 'aven't got time for a Murray Mint."

She smiled and shook her head. I raced down the bank on the path to the road. If I had turned back I would have seen my mum standing and holding the gate with both hands. The smile was still there, but her eyes always gave away her feelings. She was worried for me. But why? Today was brilliant. What could spoil it? Peter and Mark could.

Three minutes later I was down the entry between the terraced houses, into Mark's backyard, banging on the door. The door opened. A serious, moody Mrs Lamb answered.

"Is Mark in?" I said, all smiles and twitchy, energy desperate to escape.

"Did you pass?" she asked, looking down her nose at me.

"Yes. Great isn't it!"

"You're obviously very pleased with yourself." Her sarcasm was lost on me, but turning her back wasn't. She disappeared into her kitchen, leaving me standing there.

"Is 'e in?"

"No."

"Is 'e playing out?" I tried one last time.

"Try Peter's." There was a definite 'go away' sound to her voice now. I went. Miserable cow, I thought as I pushed through the gate, back down the entry.

"And close the gate!"

"Ah shut up, I 'ave done," I said quietly.

From Mark's house I carried on up the hill, past Aunty Joan's house. I ran so that if by chance she was looking out of the front room window she might not see me. I kept on running, but then felt guilty about not calling to tell her. I stopped, turned and ran back down to her house, promising myself that I would only stay for five minutes. Aunty Joan never used her front door except when guests were leaving so, as on every other time I visited, I walked down the side path between the end semis and prepared to be quiet. I softly opened the gate and immediately saw Uncle Thomas working in the rose bushes. Walking on tip-toes across the small, blue-tiled yard I slipped unnoticed through the open kitchen door.

"It's me. Anybody 'ere?"

No reply. I turned left into the sitting room. No-one here either. I walked into the hall. No use looking in the parlour because it wasn't Sunday night so they wouldn't be in there. The room was for after chapel only.

"'Elloooo," I called up the stairs.

"'Ello Joe," Aunty Joan said, popping her head out of the bathroom doorway.

"I've passed."

Her face lit up. It was important.

"Oh wonderful, wonderful."

She walked along the short landing to the back bedroom and

knocked on the window.

"Thomas, Thomas!"

No response. She rapped again, louder, "Thomas, Thomas!"

Once again she used that funny half-yodelling voice that only old aunties can do.

Thomas looked up, "Uh?"

"It's Joe, 'e's passed," she mouthed at the window.

"Uh?"

"Oh come in," signalling this time.

He did. In fact he always did as he was told.

"Joe, come up 'ere a minute."

I ran up the stairs, careful not to step on the newly painted edges and making sure I didn't kick the stair rods that kept the centre carpet in place. I'd done that once before and really got a telling off from Uncle Thomas. I stood next to Aunty Joan looking out of the back bedroom window. You could see the cottages from here. We lived in the end one at the top. In fact, the fronts of the cottages faced us now, overlooking the gardens. But no-one ever used the front doors, we all used the back doors from the kitchen. When you looked from here you could see that four of the cottages had been added in stages to the original one, which was where Aunty Connie lived next to us. That had been my grandparents' cottage where six girls and one boy had been brought up.

"Eeh, they would 'ave been proud. Fancy one of us going to the Grammar School."

I saw her eyes go misty at the thought of her parents. Do you still miss them when you are old? I suppose you must do.

"Right, come and tell us about it."

We turned and walked down the stairs just in time to see Uncle Thomas straighten his waistcoat and reach into the cupboard. It was time for the Murray Mint!

"Go on, sit down here," he pointed.

"Let 'im tell us first," Aunty Joan said.

"No, it'll calm him down."

"He's all right, aren't you?" she said, giving my curly hair an affectionate pat.

Too late, he had the Murray Mint in his hand.

"Here, try for five minutes and I'll time you." Uncle Thomas pulled the watch from his waistcoat pocket and we were off. So for the next four and a half minutes I sat on an upright dining chair in the middle of the room. I sucked the Murray Mint as was expected, when every kid knew that they tasted better when you crunched them and they stuck in your back teeth. All the while I was watched intently by Aunty Joan and Uncle Thomas. It was like feeding time at the zoo.

"Ah, aaah," he said, shaking his head as I prepared to crunch. Aunty Joan waited patiently, rolling her eyes when he looked away, making me grin.

"Ah, aah. Quietly," he admonished.

I played this game because Uncle Thomas had once had electric shock treatment for his nerves before he took early retirement, and I think that in his own way he thought he was helping me. But when you're ten years old, sitting still for five minutes is enough to send you mad by itself.

"Gone!" I felt triumphant as I stuck my tongue out for inspection. "I've passed. Jessie knew."

"They always do," Joan nodded to Thomas. He nodded back.

"I know. Great isn't it. Anyway, I 'ave to go now." I jumped off the chair. "I want to see my friends. See if they've passed."

"All right, love. Off you go. Oh, are you coming for a bath tonight?" Aunty Joan asked.

"Yes, see you later."

"Slowly."

"Leave 'im alone, Thomas. 'E's full of it."

"Doesn't hurt to slow down a bit."

"Isn't it lovely for 'im! What a wonderful school 'e's going to. I do love those striped blazers. I wonder if 'e'll get to university. I bet Ronald Clowes has passed. Oh, I can't wait to tell them at chapel on Sunday."

Her eyes went misty again, and Thomas saw it. He held her hand and sighed. He would have loved to have been a dad, and Joan would have been a good mother. It broke his heart that out of all the sisters to have married, she was the only one not to have become pregnant

Up the hill a bit further I went, across the road to Peter's house.

Don't knock at the front door. Don't *ever* knock at the front door. It wasn't boarded over from the inside like ours, it was simply never used, and Mrs Dutton used to rant and rave to "come round the back" if anyone ever made the mistake of knocking on it. So I went down the path at the side of the house, past the ankle high window that shed light into the cellar.

"What do you want?" the voice shouted from below.

Christ! I wish she wouldn't do that. I went down on my knees to look into the cellar. "'Ello Mrs Dutton. Is Peter in?" She was surrounded by washing. Every day was washing day for her. Serves her right for having six kids.

"No 'e's not, an' I bet I know what you've come for."

"I've come to play."

"Well, you'll be disappointed because 'e's out."

"Mrs Lamb said 'e was 'ere."

"She's wrong."

Then I heard voices in the big shed. Actually the shed was huge. There were three garages underneath, not that they had a car though. Baldy Dutton couldn't drive. He was a bus conductor, but couldn't drive. I thought that was funny anyway, but Peter said he didn't want to drive, something about a busman's holiday. My mum said they couldn't afford a car and that they only lived in that house because it was left to them by an old uncle of hers, and that there was something odd about why he had left it to her anyway. Still, the shed above the garages was massive, more like a barn, and I could hear Peter and Mark talking.

"Okay, ta ra," I said to Mrs Dutton, as if I believed her. I took four steps backward and then ran forward and jumped over the length of the cellar window, landing quietly so the old sod didn't know I was still there. Then I went up the stairs to the shed, and opened the door. The first face I saw was Peter's.

"Did you pass?" he scowled as he asked me. Peter was always moody.

"Yeah! What about you?"

"No." He turned away.

Mark was hanging from one of the rafters, facing the door.

"What about you, Mark?" I asked.

"Yep!"

"Aaah! Brilliant!" I ran to him and hugged him.

"He's lying," Peter spat out as he picked up a hammer and began banging on his dad's workbench

I dropped my arms from round his waist and looked up at Mark's face. "Are you?"

He nodded, dropped to the floor, and burst out laughing to the sound of Peter's hammering.

"Oh well," I said, "the schools are right next door to each other."
Bang. Bang

"So what? You won't be speaking to us," Peter said. Mark just stared. Bang. Bang. Bang.

"Why not?"

Bang. Bang. Bang.

"Because you're a snob now."

Bang. Bang. Bang.

"No I'm not."

"You will be."

Bang. Bang. Bang.

"Why should I?"

"Because you think you're better than us now. Anyway, sod off. You 'ave to go now because me and Mark are playing inside and me mum says only two can come in."

"Liar!" I shouted before he could start banging again.

Now the hammer was pointed at me. "Don't call me a liar, Harrison."

"Liar! Your mum never allows anyone into 'er 'ouse because she's always got washing lying around."

"Well, she is today and you're not coming in. An' watch what you're saying about me mum."

He threw the hammer back with the other tools lying in the wood shavings.

"But we arranged to go to the big swing." I switched to look at Mark. He just stared.

"That was yesterday. Today's different."

"It's not today that's different. It's you that's different."

"I said '*sod off*.'"

"Awr, come on, we can still be friends."

"Get lost, Joey boy"

"What about you, Mark? Why aren't you saying anything?" All he did was stare. Then he flipped his nose with his forefinger, the sign for a snob.

"Sod you then. Pair of idiots," I said.

"Don't call me an idiot, Harrison," Peter said, squaring up to me.

"Why not? You're acting like one."

"Bighead!"

"Get stuffed, both of you."

I slammed the shed door behind me and banged down the wooden stairs. The door opened behind me.

"If you slam this door again, you're dead."

"Get lost."

"Get lost to you as well."

"'Ey, I thought you'd gone?" came the voice from the cellar.

"'And you can sod off as well," I thought. I didn't like what had happened. It wasn't a nice feeling when your friends turned their back on you.

I walked back down the road from Peter's to the corner shop. Maybe those new sweets, the Magic Wands, had come in. Peter and Mark weren't my best friends, but now it seemed they weren't my friends at all. Sod them, maybe Barry would be in. I'd call after I've been in the shop. Barry already went to the Grammar School so I knew he'd be pleased. I crossed the road to the shop, and then I saw them through the shop window, looking at me. I was too late to turn away.

"'E's coming in. You ask 'im," Betty the shop owner said.

"Like 'ell I will. I don't care if 'e 'as or 'asn't," Vera replied to the window. Vera was Betty's younger sister and last year her son Roger hadn't passed. She'd complained to the school, said he was bright enough and there'd been a mistake. Anyway, Roger was now in the top class at the Secondary Modern School and "sure to be transferred when 'e's thirteen".

"You bloody well do," Betty said, hands on hips and frowning at the lie

"'Ave the Magic Wands come in yet, Mrs Drake?"

"Should be this afternoon, Joe. 'Ave you passed?" Betty asked.

"Yeah. Me mum's really pleased."

"It'll be 'ard ye'know," Vera said to the window, refusing to look at me. "Do you think you're good enough?"

"Must be, otherwise I wouldn't 'ave passed," I said honestly, not knowing what else to say, and not recognising the put down.

"There you are. Cocky already. 'Appens to 'em all. They get to the Grammar and it goes to their 'ead."

"Give over. 'E's not even 'ad a day there yet, 'ave you, Joe?"

"You mark my words, 'e'll be another big 'ead like the others," Vera said, refusing to give in.

"Your Roger's a big 'ead and 'e only goes to the Secondary."

Oh Christ! Now why did I say that? Betty put her hand over her mouth, and patted her fat tits with the other. She was always over-dramatic. Vera nearly turned me to stone with her stare.

"You cheeky little bugger. I'll tell 'im what you said. See 'ow cocky you are then."

I'd had enough, I turned and walked out.

"Go on, get off, you're just like your mother, all mouth. An' don't bloody well come back for any Magic Wands, because there won't be any for ye'," she added.

"Hey you, don't be turning my customers away," Betty said, her tone obviously serious.

"On 'is side are ye'? All you bloody well think about is money. You're me sister. You should be on my side."

I walked past the window and glanced inside. I was forgotten about.

"I've got a business to run, and I'm not 'aving you turning customers away."

"You 'eard what 'e said about my Roger."

"So what? We all know Roger's a big 'ead."

"*What* did you say?"

"I said—"

"I 'eard what you said. And what about your Keith? 'Ey, what about 'im? If you ask me 'e needs a girl round 'im and fast. And we all know what I mean by that"

"Now you watch your mouth, Vera—"

I didn't hear the rest I was too far away, I was headed towards Barry's. He lived in a massive house. Five bedrooms, two staircases, orchard, go-kart. Aunty Joan had told me that when Aunty Elizabeth was a young girl she had been a maid at the 'big house' and lived-in, but that had been when people 'with money' had lived there. I walked down the long poplar tree lined drive and went to the back door.

"Is Barry in, Mr Deakin?"

He was tall, had a fat stomach, a Charlie Chaplin moustache, and a friendly face.

"Hello Joe. No he's not, he's at his granddad's today, staying for tea as well. But I expect he'll be playing tomorrow though."

"I've passed, you know."

His face beamed. "Well done, Joe, well done! Here, shake my hand. I bet your mum and dad are pleased."

"Yeah," I grinned. Actually my dad was on six-two so he didn't know yet, but I thought it was all right to say it.

"Wait here, Joe."

He quickly went inside and came out a moment later with his old tweed jacket with the leather patches on the elbows. He was holding it up with one hand, while his other hand reached into one of the side pockets and came out with a fistful of change. He examined what was there and gave me the biggest coin. Half a crown! "There you are. Treat yourself. You must have worked hard."

Two and six! Even when I had done all my errands on Saturdays for my aunties and had my pocket money it was never that much. I stared at the half a crown in my open hand. "Thanks," was all I could say. It was such a surprise.

"Go on, off you go and spend it at Betty's. See you tomorrow, Joe."

"Yeah, see you tomorrow."

I tucked the coin deep into my pocket but knew for a fact that I wouldn't spend a penny of it in Betty's corner shop. She could keep her Magic Wands after what Vera had said.

I was really pleased now and so I decided to go to the big rope swing on my own, sod Peter and Mark. I thought about which way to go and chose the High Street. It was the longest way, but definitely safer if you were by yourself. Through the council estate was okay if you had others with you, that way the gangs on the estate probably wouldn't bother you. The shortest way was through the backs and across the I.C.I. playing field to the Drumber, but that way was never safe. Virginia Gale's gang controlled the playing field, trees, and stream this side of Dingle Lane. No-one went that way even with mates. Virginia was fifteen and had the toughest gang on the estate, but her territory stopped at Dingle Lane, and across the road in the Drumber anyone could play. That was where the big swing was. Someone had climbed the big oak tree on the top of the steep bank to the stream, and if you ran hard enough along the edge of the bank before taking off in an oval flight it was possible to be hanging forty foot in the air over the Drumber valley at the best point. It was brilliant and a real test of nerves.

I walked down the High Street and when I reached the old post office I stopped and looked straight across the road to my new school, the Winsford Verdin Grammar School. Actually I'd walked past it every day for the past five years because Winsford County Primary, my current school, was the next-but-one building, and between the two was the Secondary Modern. Today it looked different though — special but not something I couldn't have — and soon I would be wearing a striped blazer, just like Miss Andrews had said I would if I worked hard.

Right outside Jasper's shop was the zebra crossing with its belisha beacons where all the kids crossed the High Street to go to school, but today I stayed on Jasper's side. My mate, Graham, was really lucky because he lived in the terraced house next to Jasper's, and he only had to get up at a quarter to nine every day for school. My mum had said that all these houses were going to be knocked down to make way for a new shopping centre.

"Why?" I had asked.

"It's to do with the overspill people on the new estates."

"What new estates?"

"Well, the Ponderosa for a start, and there's going to be some more behind Swanlow Lane."

"Why is it being called after the ranch in 'Bonanza'?" I thought my mum was joking now and I smiled.

"It's not. It's just what Winsford people 'ave called it because it will be so big. It's proper name is the Grange Estate."

"Why, 'ow big is it?"

"When it's finished it will cover all the fields from the other side of the High Street to St John's Church and might even go as far as Knight's Grange farm. It's a disgrace building over all those lovely fields."

"But Winsford already 'as big estates. The Dene Estate, and Wharton Estate. What difference does it make anyway?"

"Stop arguing. It's not the same."

"You said that you used to play in the fields where they built the Dene Estate, and it shouldn't 'ave been built. Are you saying that it's all right now? You never liked it before."

"At least it's got Winsford people on it."

"Well, why can't we move on it? Then we'd 'ave a bathroom and toilet inside."

"We're not living on a council estate and that's that. There's nothing wrong with the cottages. They were good enough for us when we were kids and they're good enough for you."

"Anyway, what about the Wharton estate? You don't even like people from Wharton. You've always said that, and now you're saying —"

"Now you shut up. Your dad's from Wharton."

"You don't like 'is family anyway."

"I'll give you a flop in it if you carry on."

I decided that the threat of the back of her hand across my mouth was real and changed tack. "Well, who's going on the Ponderosa then?"

"Overspill people from Liverpool and Manchester, but mainly Liverpool."

"The Beatles are from Liverpool, and a lot of other groups as well. The people are called 'Liverpudlians'," I said, showing that I knew about Liverpool.

"Yes, but the people coming 'ere are from the really rough parts that are being knocked down, and they're called 'Scousers'. We don't want them 'ere. Why spoil Winsford?"

"Isn't Wharton 'aving any new estates?"

"One small one. They should 'ave the whole lot, for what difference it would make up there."

"But Wharton's still part of Winsford."

"You don't understand and that's that!" she said, and that *was* that. But it worried me. I liked my town and I didn't want it spoiled by Scousers. I wondered what they would be like.

Now I looked up the steps into the darkness of Jasper's old shop and decided there and then to buy some sherbet, some liquorice root and a glass of pop.

"Which pop?"

"Mixture."

"Come on, tell me, I 'aven't got all day."

Jasper was always grumpy, but in a friendly way. The shop was empty apart from me, so I knew he had plenty of time. But it was never empty on school days, because this was the tuck shop for all three schools, and Jasper only sold sweets and pop.

"I'll have Tizer, Dandelion and Burdock, and Orangeade, four liquorice roots, and a quarter of sherbet please."

I put the half crown on the counter and sat back on the sloping chest while he mixed the drink, savouring the moment, because only big 'uns could sit on the chest on school days. Little 'uns had to stand. That was the rule. Not Jasper's rule, but a rule all the same.

"Which one then?" he asked as if he was telling me off.

"Grammar."

He grinned and measured the sherbet on the old scales.

"Well done, lad, and make sure you work 'ard. Don't be like those lazy buggers from Middlewich and Northwich."

"Definitely not."

I gulped the pop, slid down the chest, grabbed my change, and with a clown's smile in Dandelion and Burdock round my mouth I emerged into the bright sunshine.

"See you, Jasper," I called back as I looked up the steps into the darkness.

"Mr Buckley to you, ye' cheeky bugger."

I grinned, turned and bumped straight into a woman who was walking past with her daughter. I didn't recognise them.

"Oh! I'm really sorry, I wasn't looking where I was going."

"Don't worry, luv," she smiled, and carried on walking. Her daughter laughed and I felt embarrassed because she was only about seven and I was ten. I watched her walk past, she had long blonde hair and it looked really nice in the sunshine. Then it dawned on me how the woman had spoken — she was from Liverpool! They were Scousers! But they were nice and friendly, the woman was nice looking and so was her daughter. I watched them as they walked up the High Street, chatting away to each other, the girl saying something about her dog and her mum telling her not to worry because Patch would be all right in the removal van with her dad. The girl must have realised that I was still looking and she turned, smiling. I smiled back. Then they were gone. They were nice, I thought, I don't see what the problem is all about.

"Ey, 'aven't you gone yet!" the voice growled.

"Christ, Jasper you made me jump!" He was standing at the top of his steps

"An' less of that bloody swearin', or I'll be round to see your dad."

"You don't know 'im."

"Don't I? Go on, bugger off."

I decided to bugger off.

Looking at Graham's house I had thought my mum was wrong. They would never knock down all these houses or the Swan pub, because most of the High Street would have to go. But I was wrong, they did.

I turned right into Dingle Lane, crossed over by the Rechabites Rest, down past the doctors' surgery and I was there. The Drumber swing. I looked over the fence. Great! No-one was there, I had it all to myself. I squeezed through the gap in the fence and went to the top of the bank. I pulled the bag of sherbet from my pocket and sat down. I wasn't going to mess about dipping my finger into it because I needed the energy fast, so I decided to pour. I filled my mouth until my tongue was covered with the sharp tasting crystals, and then lay back and stared at the sky while I moved the sherbet round and round until it had all dissolved. Now, to work.

I slid down the bank to catch hold of the thin piece of washing line attached to the big knot at the end of the rope. Without this it was impossible to reach the rope, because it came to rest so high off the ground. I went back up to the top of the bank and started slowly to build up my confidence. First go, butterflies in my stomach. Second go, wanted to pee. Third go, all the way out.

Now I was swinging as far out as the teenagers did when they were showing off to their girlfriends. After a dozen or so goes I sat and had one of the liquorice roots. I needed a rest from hanging on so tight. I had exactly ten minutes. I know that because I timed it once at home. From working all the way down the bark to chewing the centre of the liquorice root into a yellow stringy soggy mess took ten minutes. I was ready again.

Now for one-handed! But first I needed a pee. Probably nerves, but here goes. Little jump at first using my best hand, right one of course. My grip slipped and I fell off almost as soon as I left the bank, hit the slope and rolled down to the stream, luckily stopping short of the water. Dirty and very shaken I scrambled up the bank and looked round to make sure that no-one had seen me. They hadn't. I had another go, left hand this time. It was a good one and I managed to hold on all the way round. I didn't push my luck and went back to two hands. Normally we gave out 'Tarzan' screams when we took off, because it sounded brave and was okay to show off. But when you were by yourself it seemed childish so I didn't.

Confidence now fully restored after the fall I set myself up for a really big one, took a mighty run, and launched myself off the edge. As my feet left the ground I heard him shout.

"Right you big 'eaded little bastard. What did you say to me mum in the shop? I'm going to 'ave you for that."

I jerked my head round as I swung out, but I already knew who it was. Roger Palfreyman. But I shouldn't have turned my head, because it made me spin, and as the thick rope carried me round in a big oval I turned more and more. Roger stood on the bank with his hands on his hips.

"I'm going to show you what we do to big 'eaded Grammar Grubs," he shouted at the top of his voice. I was turning all the while the swing carried me out over the stream at the highest point. First I could see him, and then I was looking across to the other side of the Drumber valley. At first there was just him, but with each turn others appeared through the gap in the fence: Peter, Mark, thick Dave (definitely Secondary Modern gardening class material), and then two other bigger ones I didn't know, probably Roger's mates from school.

I was scared. Really scared. I thought about letting go and trying to run off, but I was so high up it scared me even more to let go. I wished with all my heart I hadn't had such a perfect run-up to the launch, but I had, and when I took off the rope had started out in a perfect oval swing. The trouble with the perfect oval swing was that it took you right back to where you started, right where Roger was now standing with his fists clenched and his right arm was out ready to punch me as I came in to land.

"Smack 'im in the face," Peter shouted, as I started the final quarter of the oval.

"Get out of the soddin' way. I want a good shot at 'im," Roger barked at Mark. They all stood back as I came in to land. All except Roger.

My heart was pounding and I felt like I was going to pee myself. He stood there, right in the way, ready to punch me, and the others were ready to join in. Still turning I held on tight and pulled my legs up so that I made a tight ball. The punch glanced off the side of my head, stinging, but not as hard as I thought it would. It wasn't hard enough to stop me swinging or turning, and with my legs off the ground I kept on moving.

"You lucky little shit. Now you're for it."

Roger lunged at me while the others watched, but the rope turned me, and as he punched again I kicked out with both legs, missing with my left but hitting his chin with my right. His head jerked up and he yelled, but he kept chasing along the top of the bank as the rope prepared to take me over the edge again.

His eyes blazed as he ran and I kicked out wildly while I held on for grim death. I shouldn't have kicked! He caught my leg, slowing my swing, and then managed to grab round my waist just as the rope took me over the edge of the bank. He wouldn't let go.

"Get off, get off, you stupid bastard idiot! We'll both fall off," I yelled, but the shit wouldn't let go. He'd rather hurt himself than let me go. We started to swing out and I knew I couldn't hold us both for long so I took a chance and let go with my right hand and stuck my thumb in his eye and pressed. He screamed, his hands lost their grip, and he fell. I quickly grabbed the rope with both hands again and looked down in time to see him hit the side of the bank, scream again, then roll down into the stream.

"'E's killed 'im," Peter shouted.

I started to cry with fear.

"Quick, down the bank."

They all jumped over the edge of the bank and scrambled down towards him. He was still screaming when they reached him.

My hands felt sweaty, but fear made me grip tighter because through my tears I could see I was now at the highest point. Roger had only fallen from ten feet and look what had happened to him. Please let me hold on, please let me hold on, I kept saying to myself. And let them forget about me.

Peter was the first to him.

"Oh shit! What a mess 'e's in. Look at 'is face."

Roger started crying, "Me arm, me arm."

"Oh God," Mark said, "it shouldn't bend there, should it?"

"Get the bastard for me," Roger cried. They looked up at me on the swing.

"Stay with 'im, Dave, we're going for Joey boy."

"Get 'im," I heard them all shout as they started back up the slope.

My heart was thumping as I came in to land. I hit the ground running and made it to the gap in the fence before they reached the top of the bank. I ran straight across the road and over the fence on the other side. This time I had to take the short cut home, and just hope that Virginia Gale and her gang were not in the woods. I followed the path down through the trees out of sight of the road, and I was about a quarter of the way across Virginia's territory when I heard Peter shouting.

"'E must have gone that way. 'E's not running either way along

Dingle Lane or we'd see 'im."

"'E's mad. If Virginia finds 'im, 'e's 'ad it," Mark said.

"Same if we catch 'im, so what's the difference, clown?"

"Who do you think you're calling a clown?" Now Mark was squaring up to Peter. "And who said you were the leader?"

"Knock it off, you two," one of Roger's mates from school said. "We're supposed to be after 'im, an' 'e's getting away. I say we go straight after 'im. Virginia goes to the Secondary, so she won't get us."

All the time they talked I kept running and glancing back, knowing that soon they would start chasing again. The path started to rise out of the hollow and the trees, which meant that I would have to break cover. I was now halfway across and scrambled up the last part of the hollow head down and on all fours. Then the shadow appeared.

"Who the fuck are you?" It was a girl's voice.

I looked up, straight up the skirt of Virginia Gale.

"What the fuck d' you think you're doing in my territory?"

She stood with her legs straddling the path I was climbing up. My eyes were now level with her feet. I didn't stop staring, I just kept looking up. Her gang appeared around her. I kept staring. I could see right up her skirt and she wasn't wearing any knickers!

"Don't move," she said, grinning. "And what are you staring at?" her voice now threatening.

"Nothing," I said, dropping my eyes.

"Look up!" she ordered. I did and my eyes followed her dusty feet in old stilettos, over her muscley young legs and back up her skirt to the blonde hair. She breathed in and raised her elbows in a threatening stance, and as her hands lifted slightly, so did her skirt. She moved her hips forward in a more aggressive stance and allowed me to see her full shape. The fine blonde hair was transparent and my stomach and balls tightened. It was my very first sighting. Now I knew why she controlled a gang made up solely of boys.

"What the fuck are you doing 'ere?" she now demanded.

"I was on the big swing in the Drumber and a gang of Grammar Grubs set on me," I lied to save my life.

"You don't go to our school."

"I will in September. There's five of them after me. Listen, you can 'ear them coming now." And they were. I was praying she would let me get away before they reached me and she found out I was lying to her.

"'Ow old are you?"

"Ten."

"Want to join our gang?" she said grinning, thrusting her hips forward one last time.

"Wouldn't mind."

"Fuck off, you're too young. Go on, get lost." She looked down the path into the trees, "We've got work to do."

I was racing across the field by the time the last of her gang disappeared down the path towards Peter and the others. I was a good runner, one of the best in my school, but at any time I expected a hand to grab my shoulder and pull me back.

I was at the edge of the field, nearly into Dene Drive, when I heard the shouts. Should I look? I had to. Oh Christ! Over my shoulder I saw them all come running out of the hollow, both gangs now screaming and shouting, and all after me! And the one shouting the most was Virginia.

Run faster, run faster, was all I could think. Head down, eyes watering with fear, for God's sake don't trip up, I thought. In every film I'd ever seen when the person who was being chased tripped up, no matter how far in front he was, he always got caught before he could get back up again. Why, I don't know, but it must be true because it always happened.

I headed for the backs between Hickey's Hill and Overdene. I took a quick look back. They were at Dene Drive. They were gaining on me. I went between Dene Street and John Street backs, now they were at Hickey's Hill. But when I got to Well Street backs and looked, they had gone.

"Oh God!" they must be cutting through Overdene orchard to head me off. I couldn't run any faster and tears of fear were making my eyes blurred as I ran along the narrow backs, finally bursting out into Lower Haigh Street. This was the finishing line, the ambush point. No fist hit me and there were no shouts. I'd beaten them. I ran up past Betty's corner shop, across the road and up the path to the cottages.

Lassie was sitting at her usual spot against the wall of number one. She could see anyone coming up the path from there, and she stood and wagged her tail when she saw me. I ran and knelt and hugged her. I stopped crying and wiped my face. "That was close,

Lassie, very close." She licked my cheek.

"Joseph! Is that you?" I heard my mum shout. Always Joseph, never Joey, that was a budgie's name.

"Yeah." How the hell did she know I was here, I thought

"Well, wherever you've been your dinner was ready two hours ago. Now get in."

Together me and Lassie walked up past the small back yards of the cottages to our gate.

"Ha, ha, haaa."

Lassie growled.

"Careful Lassie, she could turn you into a frog."

"What did you just say?"

"Nothing Mum. What's for dinner."

"Sandwiches."

"They 'aven't gone cold have they?"

"Hey, get in, wash yer 'ands, and watch yer lip. You as well, Lassie, get in. And where did you say you've been?"

"Swinging through the jungle like Gordon 'Tarzan' Scott, then outrunning a marauding gang of restless natives." Oh, and I also saw up Virginia Gale's skirt and she doesn't wear knickers. Actually I didn't say that bit.

"Gordon Scott isn't the real Tarzan, Johnny Weismuller is."

"Johnny Weismuller is fat."

"'E was an Olympic swimmer."

"'E's fat in every film I've seen 'im in."

"Get in and wash yer 'ands."

"Yes, Jane."

"Hey! In. You as well," she said, looking down at Lassie. We walked through the gate, both wagging our tails. Me because I was safe, and Lassie because she was a dog and always wagged her tail.

I didn't recognise the knock on the door later that night so I looked through my bedroom window. Nothing. Whoever it was must have been standing right next to the door, just out of sight. I wanted to open the window to see, but that would have been nosy, just like the witch, and I wasn't going to be compared to her. So I listened. The person knocked again, and if a knock could be bad-tempered, this was it. The second knock started Lassie off barking.

She didn't like the sound of it either.

I went to the top of the stairs just in time to see my dad walk past from the front room to the kitchen.

"Who is it, Dad?"

"I don't know, an' it's always when I'm watching summat on the telly."

He'd been in a good mood all afternoon, and when I'd told him I'd passed I could tell he'd been pleased, even though he didn't say much. He never asked about school, but when he was in his garden he did talk about his flowers and his show birds. So I'd told him in the garden, just like mum said, where I'd been helping him after he came in from work. He'd said "Good," smiled, and we'd carried on gardening. I hadn't told him about what else had happened today because he was telling me about some new British birds he was getting for the aviary next week, and I would be taking them to their first show next Saturday. Whenever there was a show on and he was working earlies he would put the birds in their show cages before he left for work in the morning and then I would take them in their large carrying cases to the hall where the show was, put them out for the judging, and then he would arrive just before the judging started at three o'clock. Judging was always at three o'clock. If the show was in Middlewich, one of his work mates from a different shift would meet me off the bus to make sure I found the right place. I liked the shows because it was one of the few things me and my dad did together.

When the person knocked for the third time, my dad was annoyed. I ran down the stairs two at a time.

"All right, all right. Give us a chance." He flicked the latch and pulled the door open. Outside stood an old woman. I could tell my dad didn't know who it was from the way he didn't say anything. But I recognised her. She was Roger's grandmother, and now I wished I'd told my dad what had happened today.

"About time an' all," the old woman said through yellow teeth. "Is your lad in?"

"And who are you?"

"Mrs Jones to you, Vera Palfreyman's mother, Roger's grandmother. An' our Roger's in 'ospital because of your lad. 'E ought to be chained up, the violent little bugger. 'An ye'd better keep that bloody dog away from me as well. Noisy, yappin' thing."

My dad turned to look at me. He wasn't pleased. When he

frowned and his eyebrows met he looked frightening.

"Get 'old of Lassie."

I did, but she kept growling at the old woman. Lassie could sense that she was nasty.

"What's the matter, Sam?" my mum said, coming out of the front room. She glanced to me as she stood there holding my little sister back, who had followed her.

"I'm finding out now if ye'll keep quiet."

"I only asked," my mum said, "and what does she want?"

"That's what I'm finding out."

"You'd do well to listen to yer 'usband and shut up. That lad of your is a big 'eaded little trouble maker, an' 'e'll get what's coming to 'im. Mark my words 'e will."

The voice was cutting and I could tell it had taken my mum by surprise. Then my mum started.

"Well it won't be from you or your Vera. Take yer 'ook and go. Don't listen to 'er Sam, that family's just jealous, that's all. I knew it would 'appen when Joe passed."

"Shut up, Vi," my dad said, surprising us.

"That's right, you shut 'er up and listen."

The old woman's face was frightening as she narrowed her eyes into thin slits and pointed a wrinkled finger at me.

"Our Roger's in 'ospital because of 'im."

I ducked behind the wall and sat on the stairs. My mum looked at me, and I could see she was now worried, wondering what was coming next. My little sister began to cry, softly at first, and Lassie started growling again, showing her teeth to the old woman's raised hand. Lassie jumped forward and snarled, not taking her eyes off her.

She stepped back frightened, but her face grew blacker.

"Keep that bloody dog off me or I'll 'ave it put down!"

I screamed and ran to Lassie, holding her to stop her growling. I was now in full view of the old woman.

"Yes, you little bugger, I bet you've told a lovely tale to yer mam and dad, an' I bet they fell for it —"

"'E's said nothing," my dad interrupted.

"Well then," she folded her arms to make a point, "it shows 'e's got something to 'ide, doesn't it?"

"No, I 'aven't Dad, 'onest. I'll tell you what 'appened."

"No!" she shouted, "I'll tell you what 'e did. 'E almost gouged out

Roger's eye before 'e kicked 'im off the Drumber swing, making 'im fall forty foot into the stream. 'E could 'ave killed 'im. As it is our Rogers in 'ospital with a broken arm and a patch over 'is eye."

"Dad, Dad," I pleaded, "they came to beat me up. It's not like she said."

"You little liar! 'E'd been cheeky to our Vera in the shop and then 'e was making fun of Roger and the others saying that only idiots couldn't pass their exams for the Grammar School. An' when Roger went to 'ave a go on the swing with 'im, 'e did that to 'im. Said the swing was only for Grammar kids. That lad of yours isn't right in the 'ead."

She stared such an evil stare that I started to cry, and my sister started crying louder.

"Dad, Dad. It's not true. They started it."

"So it 'appened did it?"

"Not like that, Dad, 'onest."

I was holding Lassie tight, and now she started to growl at my dad because of the way he was looking at me.

"No, Lassie, no."

"Up the stairs now," he yelled at me.

I could feel myself wet my pants.

"'E needs a good thrashing," the old woman said, sounding happy with herself.

"Enjoying this are ye, ye evil bitch," my mum said to the old woman who was smirking as she turned and left.

The door slammed shut.

"You're not 'itting 'im till we know what 'appened," my mum said.

"Move! 'E's not fighting, and 'e's not calling people idiots because they don't go to the Grammar School."

"You're not touching 'im!"

She stood in his way.

When he pushed her aside, Lassie went for his ankle.

"Keep that bloody dog away."

He charged upstairs, unfastening the buckle on his belt as he neared the top. My sister was screaming, Lassie was barking, I was crying.

"Shut them up!" he ordered down the stairs.

He banged open the door to my bedroom and grabbed hold of me, his belt folded in two in his right hand.

"No, Dad! They came to get me."

The belt came down on my legs, and I screamed at the stinging pain.

"No, Dad, please! I'm telling the truth."

Again the belt stung.

"Yer not fighting, and yer not calling people idiots. I'm not having ye turning into a little snob because ye go to the Grammar."

"Dad, Dad! They were picking on me. Oh, please Dad, please, it was them."

Twice more it stung. I held my hands up, but it hurt worse when the belt hit my fingers. I curled up in a ball, but he lifted me and hit me more on my legs and backside.

"For God's sake! Leave 'im!" my mum shouted and grabbed hold of his arm. "That's enough. 'E's a little boy. Leave 'im!"

He stopped. His eyes stared at me, but didn't see me at first. I was sobbing and in a tight ball, expecting the next sting at any minute. He pushed past my mum and went down the stairs and outside. I heard him walk round the side of the house to the garden. My mum put her arms round me.

"'E wouldn't listen. I told the truth, they picked on me," I said as sobs wracked my body. "I told the truth. I wouldn't start a fight against five others, but she didn't say that. I told the truth and 'e wouldn't listen. 'E wanted to believe 'er. 'E doesn't like me now I've passed, I can tell."

"Shh, shh," she said, hugging me tight. "'E'll never 'it you again."

"I 'ate him. I 'ate him."

"No you don't, it just seems that way now."

"I'll never tell 'im anything again, ever," I sobbed, "because 'e doesn't want to listen. And I'm never going to tell 'im anything about school. Never, ever."

Chapter 3

I felt the pressure on my hand. My fingers were being squeezed. My eyes opened, slowly at first, taking in the surroundings as my body woke up in phases. I must have dozed off. From the starlight coming in through the window I could see my dad was still asleep. The squeezing of my hand continued and then I realised he was gripping my hand really tight. I moved slowly, soundlessly out of the chair, careful not to make a noise that would wake him. Something glistened on his cheek. It was water. His eyes were watering. His grip was still tight. He must be dreaming. I reached for a tissue to gently wipe his eyes.

Oh God, Oh God! I always knew I'd been wrong. I should've listened, I should've listened. Oh Joe, why didn't you tell me in the garden that afternoon? Why leave it 'till now? Do you think I haven't gone over it again and again in my mind? You didn't speak to me for weeks afterwards, but it changed things, didn't it.

Remember how we used to go to the pictures to watch the Tarzan and Hercules films, and then we would race back along Queensway, me on one side and you on the other. Your favourite film was "Romulus and Remus" which starred Gordon 'Tarzan' Scott and Steve 'Hercules' Reeves. We even had a fight when we got in after that one and I let you be Romulus so that you could win. Hey, and do you remember when you asked me who Kennedy was that night we went to see Paul Newman in "Hud" at the Palace cinema?

I loved going to the pictures with you, but we never went again, did we? I ruined it. Just like the bird shows. You said no.

"But why aren't ye' taking them? Yer always do."

"I just don't want to."

"But I've got the new ones to show. They came this week. I told yer about them."

"No."

"I can't show them if ye don't."

Nothing. I tried again.

"No."

The "No" wasn't nasty or bad-tempered. It was worse. It was cold.

Too cold for a ten-year-old. And it was my fault.

More tears ran down his face. I wiped them again. Should I call the nurse? Was he all right? He looked so helpless.

It was like you didn't want to know me. You shut me out. I should have picked you up and hugged you and cried for you and said how sorry I was. I should have promised you that I would always listen to you first. I should have let you see me upset. But I didn't. I had my chance but I let it go. And now it's too late.

His body shuddered and he gave out a long sigh. His eyes were still closed, but the tears were rolling down his cheeks.

"Ssh, Dad, ssh," I said as I gently stroked his forehead and brushed back his hair, still thick after all these years.

"Ssh. You relax. I'm with you Dad. Don't worry. I'm here. I'm with you."

I smiled at him.

He squeezed harder, as if responding, and then his hand started to relax. His bad dream had ended.

It's not a dream, Joe. It's real, like it was yesterday, and when something that bad happens you have to do something about it there and then. Believe me, thirty years is a long time to regret something. And the loss. Joe, the loss breaks your heart. Little boys are not little boys for long. A little girl is for life, but a little boy becomes a man, and those precious years, those oh so few precious years should be savoured. And I let them go because I couldn't hug you, because I couldn't admit I was wrong. I had become my own dad, and shut out a little boy.

When I think about my own dad, I only ever seem to remember how strict he was. Once, as a boy, I had climbed over the wall to sit in the sty with Gertie and her new piglets. He said one word "Out" and smacked me round the head. The look in his eyes making it very clear that if I cried or went in there again, I would have more of the same.

I went across the field, over the wall, and into our back garden. My ear was red and throbbing from the smack, but I didn't cry. And I didn't go into the house either. It wasn't dinner time yet and my mam didn't allow us in the house until the food was ready. She said she didn't want us 'under her feet' while she was cooking.

That's what it was like in our house when I was a boy. We were a family, me, four sisters, Mam and Dad. But there wasn't much time for each other. Everyone was always arguing or being bossy. Except me and Nettie. I liked her. She was my favourite sister.

No-one showed their love, it was soft, seen as a weakness. We were a family that was looked after, but we were brought up to be hard, that's just the way it was. If I'd been in a fight and lost, I was hit again by my dad. He said it would teach me to win in future.

So I did win. And you know what? It got worse. For every fight I won, there was someone else who wanted to have a go at me. It never stopped. There was always a fight to be had.

When I see your family now, Joe, I envy them. What a childhood! They are so affectionate and free with their love and feelings. They don't feel embarrassed about walking up to me and putting their arms around me and kissing me. You are so lucky. I wish I had had that when I was a boy. I had it for a while with you, but I threw it away with my temper. Your boy David is everything I dreamed of when I was a boy. He tells me all about school, his friends, and what he has been doing with you. He tells me everything, and I love to sit and listen. We could have been like that, couldn't we Joe, but I spoiled it. I spoiled it.

His head rolled from side to side, as if shaking, saying no. This was too much, he needed the nurse.

No! I don't need the nurse. I'll be all right.

Then the rolling stopped almost as soon as it began. I sat back again. I decided to leave it a few more minutes before I called for her.

Catherine makes me laugh. She really plays David along, but you can see the love between them. What a family. So open. They take after their mother. You made a good choice Joe. She softened you. I turned you against me, but it was the me in you that shut me out. You were hard like me. I don't mean for fighting, oh no, I knocked that out of you. And for that I have no regrets, but I couldn't stop the coldness when you shut people out. You never gave anybody a second chance, just like me. Except that I hit them. You just left them out like you didn't need them.

Your mum did her best with me and she had more influence on you, and Emma is perfect for you. I can tell she's close to you. I think she got to you as soon as you met.

I was sure he smiled then. He was still dreaming, but he was now calmer. I smiled as well.

"I love you, Dad," I said quietly.

See, look how easy it is for you now. Oh I wish I could have been like you. But it wasn't the right time, we still had a long way to go. Yet now you and your family, my family, have finally arrived. But God what a journey. I wouldn't have thought it would have been so hard to cross that river.

I hadn't even been at the Secondary Modern for a month when my first fight happened. Well, it wasn't even a fight. I was simply picked on for being from Wharton. One of the lads from Over decided that he should teach the "thick bastards from Wharton" a lesson, just to put us in our place and let us know that we were really lucky to be coming over the river to the big school. He caught me with a fist right in my mouth as I walked out of the school gates. No warning.

When I walked in from school, the blood still damp on my shirt collar, I got a slap from my mam for messing my clothes up, and later that night when my dad got home I got a clip round the ear for losing the fight, with the promise that there would be another every night until I got the lad back.

Two days later I was waiting for him. I was only eleven and scared. George, the lad who had picked on me and split my lip, was thirteen and bigger. But my dad was even bigger, and the slap off him last night convinced me it was better to face George again rather than have another slap tonight when I got home. That night at the school gates I was waiting for him.

George started shouting as soon as he saw me, but I never took my eyes off him. I never said a word, I just pointed to the field behind the school, the place where all scores were settled. He nodded and grinned

We walked side by side down the path by the Golden Lion pub which led to the field. Both of us knew it couldn't start till we were both ready, otherwise that would be cheating. George had been challenged and it had to be a fair fight. There were even rules: no kicking and when the first one drew blood the fight was over. When we dropped our coats it started.

I kicked his knee. He screamed and bent forward. I grabbed his head under my arm and with my free hand punched and punched at his face until my knuckles hurt. I let go, he was already crying. Blood poured from his nose.

I'd broken the first rule and then he broke the second.

He ran at me, making a grab at my throat, I ducked and lashed out with both fists, hitting him as hard as I could, the pain from my knuckles making me cry. I didn't stop until he couldn't stand up. I beat him for calling me stupid and a bastard from Wharton, and because I was scared of my dad.

I remember that as my first proper fight, and from there it got worse. Everyone wanted to fight me. When I left school at fifteen I was the hardest kid in the year. The trouble was, kids at school had older brothers, and they wanted a go. When you had a name and a reputation for being tough everyone wanted to have a go at taking that tag away. It never stopped.

You couldn't turn out like that Joe, life's a misery. You can't relax. Wherever you go someone wants to have you out. It's better not to fight at all, then no-one bothers you. I thought the war would have helped, but it didn't. I went away when I was eighteen and was gone for four years. People would forget me, that's what I thought. Like hell they did. But I came back tougher. A boxer. I boxed in the navy, and I came back worse than ever. I was a bad-tempered street fighter with boxing skills. What idiot had taught me that? Maybe they thought it didn't matter because I would probably get killed in the war anyway. They were wrong. When I came back to Winsford I was the worst person you wanted to stare at. But it didn't even take a stare, a glance would do. I never gave anyone the benefit of the doubt, that was how you got beaten. Hit first, ask questions later.

The worst fight was the night before I met your mum. I'd been set up as a bet. I should have seen it coming, but I didn't. We were in the snooker hall at the bottom of Winsford, just near to the town bridge. I was playing on the table in the far corner, my mates were near the door waiting for me to finish. I was leaning across the table to take a long shot when the glass came down out of the shadows of the overhead light and smashed on my outstretched hand. At first I thought my thumb had gone. I couldn't see it for the blood.

I didn't scream or shout. The only sound had been the breaking glass. By the time my mates had turned I had broken the jaw of the man with the glass with my good hand, and was squaring up to another figure emerging from the shadows. Then a pair of hands grabbed me from behind, pinning my arms back. I jerked my head backward twice into his face. I heard the crack of bone as his nose broke, and then I charged forward, him still holding me, and head-butted the other one in the stomach, but he didn't fall. My mates were running to help me and were halfway across the hall when I kicked the man in front of me. He dropped like a stone. No sound, his balls must have been squashed flat. The man on my back was bleeding on my shirt, which wound me up more. I reached behind and grabbed his hair. He pulled backward, his arms let go. He pulled again and his hair came out in tufts. He yelped, then I turned and punched fast and hard, only stopping when my mates dragged me off.

It was over. But I was badly hurt, I couldn't feel anything in my thumb. The infirmary was out because the police would be involved in this one. The three on the floor were too badly injured, and even if they kept their mouths shut, the police were sure to be looking for someone else injured in a fight that night. I went home.

"Nettie, Nettie!" I whispered.

"Eh? What?"

"Nettie, it's me."

"Sam? What bloody time is it?"

"Ssh. Ye'll wake me mam and dad."

"What d'ye want," she said, pulling the bedclothes around her.

"Can ye do summat wi' this?" I showed her my thumb.

She gasped. "Oh my God, Sam, it's bloody 'angin' off."

"Ssh. Just put a plaster on it. I need to be in work tomorrow."

"Ye've been bloody fightin' again, 'aven't ye?" Her eyes looked sad. "When will it stop, Sam? Ye can't carry on like this, luv." She started to cry.

"Dunna bloody well cry, Nettie. I need a plaster."

"Ye need someone to look after ye, that's what ye need. Oh Sam, ye 'ave to stop fightin'." She got out of bed, put her arms round me, and walked me to the kitchen. "I wish ye could meet someone and stop all this."

I could tell she meant it. I loved Nettie, but I couldn't give her a kiss or hug her. Men didn't do that in our family.

"Ye'll meet ye match one day, Sam," she said as she taped up my thumb.

Nettie was right. I did meet my match. I met your mum. In fact, I met her the next day by the Magnet picture house at the bottom of Weaver Street, bandaged thumb and all.

I can't remember what film it was. Actually, I can't even remember watching a film at all. All I remember is this good-looking woman three rows in front and about six or seven seats away to my right. I hadn't seen her before, she was from the other side of the river, the Over end of town. In them days we didn't mix much. Wharton was Wharton and Over was Over. Two villages separated by a river. Winsford only existed by the shops at the town bridge, after that it was Wharton and Over. The Magnet picture house, and the outdoor baths in the summer, were the only places where people mixed. Each to their own outside of these.

Anyway, I saw her and I decided I was going to marry her. I told my mates that night when she walked out of the pictures that she was the woman I was going to marry. They laughed. I didn't. I watched her walk up Weaver Street. She knew I was watching, I saw her friends elbow her and she turned. She looked, laughed, and turned back quickly when she saw me. But she turned once more.

For the next three weeks I waited outside the Magnet on the same day, hoping she would be there again, and four weeks after first seeing her, we went out for a walk. Soon after that it was fair to say that we were courting.

I couldn't believe that I'd landed such a catch. All I could think about was us being together. Within three months I had proposed, *and on that Sunday afternoon after your mum had said yes, we went to see my mam and dad to tell them our good news. What I had never expected was how much my mam was against us being together, and it came out in the worst possible way.*

We sat there after having a few sandwiches, just the four of us, me, your mum, and my mam and dad. I think my dad had guessed what was about to come, and he had been trying his best to keep us talking, and he was being especially polite to your mum. Perhaps that had irritated my mam even more. Still, when I eventually got round to saying we were going to get married, my mam let loose, and from that moment on acted as though your mum was not in the same room.

"Well ye not, an' that's that," my mam shouted at me. "I don't know why ye're bloody well bothering with 'er. It'll come to nothing. They're all a load of stuck-up buggers up Over. She'll drop ye when the novelty wears off. You mark my words."

My eyes flashed at her, and your mum's face went white.

"If I were ye Lizzie, I'd shut up now," my dad said.

"Well, ye're not me an' I'll 'ave my say in my own 'ouse. 'E's not bloody well marrying some bit of a girl from Over. 'E'll 'ave a proper wife from up 'ere or none at all."

"You stupid woman, can't ye see the look on 'is face. 'E'll turn 'is back on ye."

"Don't call me stupid! I know what will 'appen," my mam shouted as she stood.

"Accept 'er or lose 'im. And don't stand up to me like that."

"Never!" she said defiantly, but sitting down all the same. "I'll never 'ave 'er as a daughter-in-law. She's a bloody Methodist from across the river. She's not Church, and our Sam was a choirboy at Wharton Church. That's where 'e should be getting married. Methodist and Church should keep themselves to themselves. All this mixing is not right. It was better when we were kids an' we each kept to our own side of the river."

"That sort of talk's for old folk, not us. Do ye really want us to go back to when we were kids and the fires were burning day and night under the old salt pans. The town was filthy then. Now it's better, and people need to mix more. Times change. We don't want the old prejudices back again. These young 'uns 'ave all been

through a war, just like we did. But it's their turn now, and I'm for them getting wed. They'll be a good pair. I like 'er."

"I could bloody well see that earlier. Fluttering 'er bloody eyelashes at ye. Ye big, soft bugger."

"Now watch ye tongue, Lizzie, yer on the limit now."

"On the limit? That'll be the day. I'm the boss in this 'ouse and if ye want any more meals cooking, ye'll bloody well remember that." Her eyes were cold.

My dad shook his head and looked at your mum. "Ye're welcome in my 'ouse anytime, luv."

"Then I'll be out. If 'e marries 'er, 'e's finished with me."

"Then ye've lost ye only son." He looked at me, reached out, and patted my knee. "You did well to 'old ye tongue, son, I'm proud of ye."

It was the closest thing to affection that I can remember my dad ever showing me.

We were married at Over Methodist Chapel on the High Street one year later. Six months after the wedding my dad died. My mam spoke to your mum once after that, at the funeral.

"I'll say this once so listen up. If 'e'd died before yer wedding, ye'd never 'ave got Sam. 'Ear me? Never. So don't come to me for anything else. Ye've got my son, ye've taken 'im over the river, an' now 'e lives up Over, God 'elp 'im. But 'e's not one of ye lot, and 'e never will be. D'ye 'ear! 'E's from Wharton and 'e's Church. And ye're not good enough for 'im."

From then on, they ignored me. My mam and my sisters ignored me. I never even got a birthday card. So I turned my back on them as well, and I never visited. I took you to my dad's grave, but I didn't call to see my mam. I changed, but I couldn't change everything. I couldn't change my temper or the frustration I felt at being rejected by my own family.

We went to live with your granddad Joseph. He lived with your Aunty Connie in Haigh Street because your grandma had died when your mum was only thirteen. He was a grand old man, and he saw through my rough edges.

He knew that I had never been used to a close family, and showing my feelings didn't come easy. But he also knew that when I made my choice with your mum, I turned my back on my mam and my sisters. Even Nettie sided with them in the end. That hurt. No-one, regardless of what they might say, ever wanted to be complete-ly shut out. Maybe if my dad hadn't died so soon after the wedding we would all have made up, and your mum would not have been blamed for taking me away. But, she didn't take anyone away, I walked with her gladly.

I loved old Joseph. We got on well and I'm glad you knew him as well. I always wished I could have taken you round to show you to my dad, so I could have said, just once, "Look Dad, 'ere's my little boy." But at least Joseph had that pleasure. He loved you. You were always singing for him. He used to have you standing on the din-ner table, looking at yourself in the mirror over the fireplace, singing your little heart out. Do you remember? Your Uncle Richard is just like him now, even looks like him. I expect that's why you like him. He probably reminds you of your granddad.

Me and Richard always got on right from the very start. He was the only brother with six sisters and they adored him. Whenever he visited from North Wales they made such a fuss over him. My sis-ters had never been like that, even when I had lived at home. How lovely it must have been to have lived in a house with so much love so freely given. Still, I was part of your mum's family and was always made welcome by all the sisters. It was a good, happy fam-ily, and all the brothers-in-law got on. How else could it have been? The sisters wouldn't have allowed it any other way.

About a year after me and your mum were married, Richard came to visit, bringing his wife to stay. One night I took him out for a drink to the Top House up Wharton. It was Richard's idea, he said why didn't we visit one of my old pubs instead of going to the Bull's Head again with old Joseph. It was a mistake. The calling and the aggravation started almost as soon as we walked in the tap room. It was hard to believe we were in the same town, and yet this had been my local up to meeting your mum. I was born only eight houses away in Little Fold and yet I was treated like an outcast.

"Slumming it tonight, are we?" Charlie Brandon mocked, pur-posely knocking my arm so the pint spilled. "And who's this ye bringing to our pub?"

"My brother-in-law, so watch ye mouth, Brandon."

"Don't bother about me, Sam, I've seen worse," Richard said. And

37

he had, he'd been one of the lucky ones to get away from Dunkirk.

"Well, if it isn't little Sam! And who said ye could come in 'ere again? Ye turned ye back on us when ye married from over there. It's not yer local now. It's best ye keep away."

Sid Weedall was a stupid bastard. Tall and stupid. The type who always thought that height meant superiority, yet he hadn't got a pair of shoulders big enough to hang a coat on.

"Keep talking, Sid, keep talking. I laid ye out once, and I can do it again."

"I'd be careful what ye saying, little Sam. Look around, I bet ye don't see many friendly faces." Sid replied, unable to resist smirking.

I didn't look. "Come on Richard. I've 'ad enough. We'll go. We don't belong.

"That's right, ye don't. Ye belong over there now. Ye not one of us no more."

I knew that voice without even looking. It was Ronnie Snapes, the one who'd smashed the glass into my hand at the snooker hall. A fight was coming, I could feel it. We emptied our glasses, but they wouldn't leave it alone. Richard wasn't scared, but I was worried for him. I didn't want the sisters to think I had got him hurt. I didn't want them to blame me.

"Richard," I said quickly and quietly, "if anything starts, and it probably will, just drop to the floor and lie still."

"Ye what? I'll do no such thing. We're in this together, ye my brother-in-law."

"No Richard, this is my fight. But ye 'ave to drop to the floor. Then don't move. It won't be safe. Look at 'em, they all want to 'ave me out. That's 'ow it's always been. That's 'ow it is when ye known as a fighter. When it starts I'll 'it anything that moves. Keep out of my way."

Richard nodded, he could see it in my eyes that I was scared for him.

We put our glasses down and turned to leave. Then it happened. It was big Sid.

"I'll tell ye what always surprised me," he said loudly for all the tap room to hear, "was 'ow 'e managed to sign the marriage lines. Because when 'e was at school 'e could barely read nor write, could ye Sam? 'As she been teaching ye then, because ye were a right thick bastard at school."

"Leave it, Sam," Richard said, "we're almost at the door. Let it go."

"That's right, ye take the coward out of 'ere. 'E's gone soft. There was a time when 'e'd 'ave punched ye for just spilling 'is beer." He turned away and laughed.

That was Sid's mistake, but he wasn't the first to drop. Ronnie Snapes was. He was at the end of the bar, leaning back, both elbows propping him up, laughing.

"Drop!" I said to Richard as my fist slammed into Ronnie's jaw, breaking it for a second time. It looked like I'd hit both of them. Two people on the floor. Surprise registered for a few seconds. I reached for the back of Sid's hair with my left hand, pulling his head down backwards, kneeing him in his back, then smashing my fist into his nose and mouth. Two, three, four times. He crumpled on the floor.

Charlie Brandon and his mate, Reg, moved at me quickly. Charlie was the fastest, which was unlucky for him. I grabbed the bottle of brown ale from the table and smashed it round his ear, part of which sliced off. Blood flew everywhere. He screamed like a pig. Reg hesitated and I kicked his knee, followed by three sharp punches to the gut with a final uppercut which lifted him off his feet. He was unconscious before he hit the floor.

"Any more?" I shouted. Nothing. The tap room was quiet apart from groans.

"Come on Richard, we're going." He stood up, eyes wide open, just staring at me.

"Christ, Sam!" he murmured. "I'm bloody glad I dropped."

"Not a word when we get 'ome, promise me Richard, not a word."

"Ye've got it."

We never said a word about that night, and I never went for a drink in a Wharton pub again.

That's how it had been for me, fight after fight. It's better never to start fighting because once you do, you never stop, and you always think that you are in control. You always think that you'll never lose your temper. But you do.

When I hit you as a boy, I'd lost my temper. I didn't listen to you, I listened to that bitter old woman, and it was like all the snobbery and prejudice I'd had to put up with coming out again. I'd never been able to read and write very well at school, and I was called an idiot and made fun of. I got them back the only way I knew how, by *fighting. When she'd said you were calling them idiots it set some-thing off inside of me. I didn't want you to be a snob because you'd passed for the Grammar School, and I had to stop you fighting.*

He groaned. My drowsiness left me immediately. It was the first sound he had made all night. There were more tears, more unease. What was happening to him? I had to call for the nurse.

No, let me finish! I had to stop you fighting, you couldn't turn out like me. But I went too far. I couldn't control my temper, and I kept hitting the little boy who sang on the table, the little boy I adored. The little boy I turned away from me.

His body was heaving, he was fighting for his breath, and his grip on my hand turned my fingers white. He was choking! My free hand hit the alarm button to signal the nurse.

Chapter 4

The nurse responded immediately to the call, and within seconds the door opened quickly and silently, the bright light from the corridor momentarily silhouetting her in the doorway before she turned on the fluorescent lights in the single room. I squinted as my eyes adjusted to the sharp change in light.

"How long has he been like this?" she asked, rushing to his bedside.

"A few seconds, that's all. He seemed to be dreaming at first, just slightly restless, then he became agitated like it was a really active dream, but all of a sudden it turned to this."

Hold my hand Joe, hold my hand. I'm frightened, I can't breathe. I can't get enough air into me. Help me, help me.

I must have winced as he gripped my hand tighter. The nurse noticed.

"He's fighting all the way, isn't he," she said as she placed the transparent nose and mouth cover on his face, deftly looping the elastic round the back of his head. His chest shuddered as he fought in vain to fill his lungs. It was almost as though he was drowning in fresh air. She flicked the switch and the nebuliser came alive, the sound of the spitting and hissing of the air and moisture began to fill the room.

It's not working Joe! Tell her it's not working. I can't breathe, I'm choking. My head will explode if I can't get air soon. Joe, tell her. I don't want to die, Joe, not yet, not yet....

"It's not working. He still can't breathe."

My eyes turned from my dad to the nurse, pleading with her to do something more.

"It's working, but it just takes a few moments for the mixture to

41

ease the airways. When a panic attack takes hold it causes all the airways to constrict. It's a vicious circle. What was hard becomes harder. The more he fights, the worse it gets. He has to relax, but the natural instinct of the body is to fight for breath, and your father is strong-willed. He isn't going to let go quickly. I'm afraid tonight will be a difficult night for him."

Her voice was tinted with sadness, but also admiration. She didn't look at me when she spoke, her eyes were on my dad as she gently stroked his forehead and brushed his hair back, her soothing touch helping him to relax as the nebuliser spluttered and hissed. His grip on my hand began to ease and his chest gradually began to move in a gentle rhythm, his breathing returning to a low rasping sound. It was working at last.

"There, he should be all right now, but I won't leave the nebuliser on for long. It's better that he breathes without it while he can."

While he can! This was my dad she was talking about. He can't stop breathing. He has to keep going. Dads can't stop, no matter how old they are.

She saw my reaction. Didn't she miss anything?

"Shall we have a quiet word outside. He'll be fine now."

I looked down at him. He seemed to be sleeping.

I'm not, but do as she says. Just don't be long. I don't want to be alone, Joe, not tonight, not again. Be quick Joe....

He let go of my hand.

"See, he's asleep. We need to talk, and we don't want to disturb him."

She moved away from the bed and opened the door, waited for me to walk through, and with a final look at my dad turned off the bright lights in the room and closed the door without a sound.

She turned to look at me. I waited, not wanting to listen. She began to speak, her voice calm but sure.

"It won't get any better, Mr Harrison. Your father is dying and it is only a matter of time. The nebuliser is working now, but it may not the next time. It must be difficult for you, but it's worse for your father. I have to say that I'm amazed he has lasted so long. One of his lungs has already collapsed and he can only use about a quarter of the other one. He had a similar attack to the one he just had at tea-time whilst you were on your way to the hospital. The staff thought he was going to die, but he managed to calm himself down — goodness only knows how, but he did. He obviously wasn't prepared to die at that time. Then he managed to control it himself, this time the nebuliser controlled it. Next time, who knows?"

I looked down. I didn't want to hear this. I already knew he wouldn't get better. Why did I have to listen to this? I turned my head away from her. I was going back to the room.

"Mr Harrison, I have to finish. Believe me, this is for your father, not you. I have to tell you. Your father will die a very distressful death."

Oh Christ, how can I listen to this? My eyes closed, trying to shut her out.

"Listen to me," her voice was firm, forcing me to look at her. "His remaining lung is slowly filling with fluid, that's why his breathing is becoming shallower and shallower. There's hardly any space left for air. And it will get worse. He will feel like he is suffocating, drowning, which is really what *is* happening. His body will fight for air, he will need more air to fight with, and he will slowly suffocate. It is a distressing death for him, and also distressing for you to watch."

Tears rolled down my cheeks as I listened. She continued.

"I'm afraid, Mr Harrison, that we cannot help you. But we can help your father."

I stared deep into her eyes.

"But he's going to die?"

"Yes he is, and he will die fairly soon. However, his death can be made more comfortable for him."

I found it hard to believe that she was saying this to me.

"Dr George has very strong views in cases like these where death is the inevitable outcome. His concern is for the patient and their comfort, although the final choice is yours."

"Tell me exactly," I said.

"We will insert a needle and tube into your father's arm, connected via a control box to a relaxant. Each time the button on the box is pressed, a small dose will be administered. You will have the control box on your side of the bed."

"When will I know when a dose is needed?"

"You'll know, believe me, you will know. It all depends upon whether or not you feel you can do it. Some people can, some can't. All I can say is that this will make it easier for your father."

"He's my dad, my *dad*! I've never called him my father!" I snapped at her. The sharpness of my response registered in her eyes, and I immediately felt guilty, selfish, stupid. "I'm sorry, I didn't mean...."

"Forget it, I understand."

"Do you? Do you really understand what you're asking me to do? Are your parents both alive?"

"Yes they are."

"Then you don't understand."

"I understand perfectly how your dad will die because I've seen people die this way, and I've pleaded with their family to ease the suffering. Believe me, if I ever get the chance to help my mother or father this way, I won't hesitate to do it. I'll do it, I'll be strong for them when they need me."

"I—"

"Go and sit with him. He needs you."

I watched her walk back to her desk. She wasn't angry. Had she really just said that to me? I went back to the door and glanced once more at her. She raised her head, gave a brief smile, and carried on with her paperwork. It was just another night for her.

I stepped into the room and closed the door softly behind me, not wanting to disturb him. I hoped he was sleeping, breathing gently. No tension, no anxiety, no fighting for breath, no need for injections. I leaned back against the door, eyes closed, a tightness was gripping my own chest. Oh God, what had she asked me to do? Help him die? Kill him? Surely God hadn't expected me to do that. It was too much. I couldn't, wouldn't. I had wanted to cry out loud, to protest that it wasn't fair that a man who had once been so strong should die in such a distressing way, and that I shouldn't be asked to do such a thing. I had wanted to shout "No!" but I didn't. Instead I opened my eyes to the dimness of the room, the silent, waiting tears rolled down my cheeks, and I allowed the sound of the nebuliser and his laboured breathing to reach me.

You will do it, luv. When the time comes, you will. I know you have the strength to help me, and by God I want you to. I've never felt so frightened in my life as I did just now. My chest felt like it was being crushed and I could only get a little bit of the air I wanted. I'm surrounded by air, but I can't breathe it. The panic is terrible. Then I felt like my head would explode, my chest burned more, and the room seemed to start filling up with blocks, forcing me into a corner. I fight for air, and the blocks go back. But what about when I can't get any air? Do the blocks crush me? Is that death? Oh Joe, I'm frightened. Frightened that I can't move, frightened to die. Look after me tonight, and help me when the time comes. Please help me.

Sitting beside him, I realised I wouldn't be able to do it. Thou shalt not kill. I wouldn't. In my mind I started the Lord's Prayer.

God listen to him, please listen to him, and then tell him to help me. Give him the strength, I beg you give him the strength. He thinks he'll be helping to kill me, but I'm already dying. It's only a matter of time, but don't let me die slowly. I know I have no right to ask favours, but guide him.

Look at him now. I want to reach out and hold him again, like I did when he was a little boy, and tell him everything's all right. But it's not and he needs help that I can't give.

My prayers were simple, childlike, just like they'd always been, perhaps because I'd never learned to pray properly as an adult. Did it matter? They started the same way, always had the same ending, and the bits in the middle, well, did they help? I don't know. I prayed like a young boy because I'd stopped going to chapel as a young boy. One day my mum had said that I didn't have to go any more just to please others, so I stopped going.

Forever and ever, Amen. I slept.

Chapter 5

"Joe, are you up yet?" I heard the distant shout coming through the breathing hole I'd made in the blankets. I didn't reply.

"Joseph!" The yell lasted three stomping footsteps as my mum came up the stairs. I stayed still. Ten stomps later the latch banged up on my bedroom door and a switch clicked down. There was light at the end of the tunnel! The hollow sound of shoes on lino approached my bed. I held my breath so the monster would think no-one was under the pile of blankets.

Whoosh! It hadn't worked. In one dreadful tug all the blankets were on the floor, leaving me curled up in my striped 'jamas.

"Awrr, mum. I was asleep."

"No you weren't, now get up for Sunday School."

"I don't want to."

"It doesn't matter what you want. You're going. Now get up!"

"I don't see why I have to."

"You 'ave to because I say so. Up!"

She turned. Hollow footsteps retreated to the door. I sat up.

"Why do I have to go every week?"

"Up now!"

"You don't go to chapel every Sunday."

Big mistake. I knew it as soon as I'd said it. She rotated on the lino. Quite an impressive turn really.

"What did you say, you cheeky little—! Do you want a flop in it? Do you?"

"No." It was a stupid question.

"Well get up then and less backchat."

She turned and with one hollow step was gone.

I got up. Shirt, tie, underpants, black short trousers and black blazer I wore at our Christine's wedding last year. Socks and shoes were downstairs. It was like a sixth school day except school was better. I liked the Grammar School.

"Where's Mary?" I asked through dribbling cornflake milk. "Isn't she going?"

"Your sister's name is Rose, and she's going this afternoon to the little ones' Sunday School."

"She doesn't like Rose, she wants to be Mary."

"She's Rose and that's that."

"It seems daft having a big Sunday School and a little Sunday School," I said to the back of her head as she carried on washing up.

"Shut up. You go to the big one after the first hour of chapel in the morning when you're at the big school. Always 'ave done." I pulled a face behind her back. "But you can go to both if you like. Is that what you want?"

I kept eating cornflakes.

"I just asked you a question," she said to the window.

"You just told me to shut up."

"Don't be clever with me. Do you want to go to both?"

"No." Another obvious answer to another stupid question.

"Oh, give over, and let 'im 'ave 'is breakfast without ye getting on at 'im," my dad said from the living room.

"Thanks Dad."

"That's right, you take 'is side," she said to the window, banging the plates. She rotated, took my bowl, and splashed it in the sink.

"I haven't finished."

"Well you 'ave now," she said as cornflakes floated to the surface. "Go in the kitchen out of my way."

"This is the kitchen, that's the living room," I pointed.

"Listen know-all, this is the back-kitchen, *that* is the kitchen," she pointed back.

"That's daft."

"That's what they're called in a cottage."

There were more plates banging.

"Why?"

"Because they are, that's why."

Well you can't argue with that, I thought. But I decided not to say it in case there was a flop on offer. It wouldn't taste too good with dirty dishwater. I went in the living room.

"Morning, Dad."

"Mmm," he said, his head in the paper.

Oh well, better than nothing. I took a pair of socks from the sideboard drawer and carried my shoes to the settee. I put on my shoes and socks slowly, then carefully began to tie the laces.

"You'd better not be late on purpose."

"Christ, mother! Stop creeping up on people!"

"What did you say? Don't you dare swear on Sunday."

"It's just that I thought you were still in the kitchen."

"Back-kitchen."

"Back-kitchen then. I didn't know you'd hovered in."

"Watch it." Her hand curled, flop-like.

"Okay, okay. I'm only joking. There's no need to be in a bad mood."

"I'm not in a bad mood."

"Yes you are. You're in a bad mood every Sunday."

"I am not, and if I am it's because of you. We 'ave this same pantomime every Sunday morning."

"Why aren't ye going?" Dad asked Mum. It took us both by surprise. Now I definitely did not say anything.

"Because I'm not," was all she managed.

"Why not?"

"Because I'm not. That's why. Anyway, I go at night."

"Are ye going tonight?"

"No."

"Why not?"

"Because I'm not."

Jesus, they were like two hamsters in a cage using the same wheel.

"Ye didn't go last week and ye won't be going next week."

"I might."

She was getting annoyed now, and I didn't know why he was doing this. I finished tying my laces. It would be better to get out now. I left. "See you Mum, see you Dad."

The newspaper slipped from my knee as I turned in the armchair.

"No ye won't and ye know it. Ye go three times a year, Christmas, Easter, and the 'Arvest Festival."

"You don't even go once."

"It doesn't matter whether I go or not. That's not the point, is it?"

"Why isn't it?" she asked, but there was no conviction in her voice.

"Because I'm not the one forcing Joe to go, am I? Every Sunday is the same. Ye make 'im get up to go to chapel, but ye don't go."

"I did when I was 'is age."

"That's not the point."

"Why isn't it?"

She was irritated now.

"Because 'e's been going every Sunday since 'e was three years old and 'e 'as the right to choose now. He's at the big school now and 'e gets 'omework every night, and at the weekends. Doesn't 'e deserve some time off? Some time to play? Or is it more important to ye that 'e gets 'igh attendance marks so that at the 'Arvest Festival prize-giving ye can sit and listen while 'is attendance is read out and 'e's given a more expensive book. That's what all this is about, isn't it? Not Joe, but ye and yer Methodist ways. Ye'll sit there and look around, and nod at whoever's watching. Basking in glory."

"That's right, bring it down to your Church prejudices against us Methodists. Just like your bloody mother always did. You're just like 'er."

"That's where ye're wrong, because I'm not. I'm like my dad."

"Really! 'Ow?"

"'Ow? I'll tell ye 'ow."

I stood up.

"This'll be good."

She placed her hands on her hips.

"My mam was like ye, except with 'er it was the choir. I 'ad to go to church every week because at Christmas and Easter she wanted people to see me singing in the choir so as people would see 'er as being God-fearing. Anyway, my dad put a stop to it when I went to the big school. 'E gave me the choice, and I left the choir. Joe's 'aving that choice as well."

"'E's going each week."

"In three week's time it'll be the 'Arvest Festival, after that 'e can make up 'is own mind."

"'E'll choose to go."

"Don't bet on it."

"'E will."

"Some weeks maybe, but I'll bet ye won't be looking round as much at next year's prizegiving when 'is attendance is read out."

"There's still Rose, she'll still be going."

Her voice was beginning to falter, and her eyes were becoming glassy

"Yes, I know she will, and eventually she'll 'ave the same choice."

I put my hands on her shoulders, her face looked sad.

"Will you still 'elp put the stage up and the trestles out for the 'Arvest Festival, though."

"Course I will. I'm not against the chapel, but I don't like the com-

petition between families and the snobbery."

"It's the same in the church," she said meekly, still defensive.

"Yes, it is. I'm not saying any different."

"We're not all like that."

"I think everyone is. And some more than others."

"There's no snobbery like with the church looking down on us."

"What about the Scousers?"

"I don't mind them coming to our chapel."

"You might not, but what about the others?"

"A lot of the others think like me."

"And a lot of them don't, Vi. Admit it."

She started to cry. I put my arm round her and we sat down on the settee.

"I don't want to admit it, Sam, because I'm ashamed of what's being said. I'm ashamed of what's 'appening. There's already been one of the Sunday School teachers leave because she won't 'ave Liverpool children in 'er class. She says they will be noisy and scruffy, and another is threatening to go if any are allowed to join."

"Let 'er go. Ye can't refuse children at Sunday School. Better off without 'er."

"If Winsford wasn't changing and the overspill coming, this problem wouldn't be 'ere."

"The problem is with the chapel. All the families go and look friendly, but they compete with their children, trying to outdo each other with fruit and vegetables at 'Arvest, with the stalls at the Christmas bazaar. Ye do it, they all do it."

"Your church is the same."

"Yes, but we're not talking about the church."

"But our chapel's lovely. We've always gone there. All my family. My mum and dad were married there, and so were we."

"Yes, but the congregation is only made up of certain families. And ye each sit in yer own part of the chapel."

"Like we've always done."

"That's right, like ye've always done. Can't ye see 'ow it is?"

"I don't see what's wrong with it. And you can't explain yourself either."

The edge in her voice was unmistakable, and it hurt. I took my arm away and stood up.

"No, maybe I can't. But I know what I see, and Joe's not being like that."

"What? Like a Methodist? Go on, say it. You 'aven't changed, you're still like them from up Wharton."

"Don't start again. Wharton/Church, Wharton/Church. There's Methodists up Wharton as well, and they're just the bloody same. They don't mix either."

"Maybe they don't, but we do."

"Rubbish. There's three chapels on the High Street. There's Over, the Primitive Methodists, and St Paul's. But ye never mix. Ye look down on the Prims, they look down on ye, and ye both look down on St Paul's. I'm telling ye, when ye three 'ave to join, ye won't know what's 'it ye."

I walked into the back-kitchen and banged the half full kettle onto the stove. Two matches snapped before I could light one. Your mum followed me in.

"It'll never come to that. It's only rumours," she said.

"Open your eyes, woman. It'll 'appen. It'll 'ave to when they widen the High Street. Prims chapel will 'ave to go."

"Nawr, it's set back from the road. Anyway, they'd never knock down a chapel just for a new road."

"'Ey, if they're building an estate all the way down to Knights Grange farm for outsiders, they won't think twice about knocking a chapel down to widen a road."

"They'll never let it 'appen."

"Who won't?"

"The chapel elders."

"What do ye think they can do?"

"They'll stop it, that's what."

Point made, hers arms folded. Typical.

"They're just old men. I bet there's not one of them under seventy. Most of them will be dead by the time the road's built. What do they care?"

"They'll do what's best."

"No, they won't. They'll do what they want. They'll suit themselves, and they won't care about anyone else."

The kettle started to whistle.

"Our Thomas isn't like that."

"He's only one. But I bet if ye asked 'im 'e wouldn't want to go to Prims."

The kettle whistled louder.

"No 'e wouldn't, but neither will 'e 'ave to. If they knock down

Prims they'll 'ave to come to us."

"What, and sit in your seats?"

The whistle screeched one last time and the top blew off over the cooker, bounced on the enamel, and landed on the carpet.

"Ye wouldn't want it and they wouldn't do it."

"Well turn it off then," she said, looking at the kettle, steam gushing out of the spout. She was glad of the diversion.

"Well?"

"Well what?"

She brushed past me and reached for the teapot, tugging at the cosy. The old cold tea was swished down the sink. The caddy surrendered fresh tea leaves, and after the boiling water was splashed into the teapot the lid was loudly clicked into place, signifying she was ending the conversation. I wasn't.

"It never ends, does it?"

"What doesn't?"

"This bloody snobbery. Wharton looks down on Over, Over looks down on Wharton—"

"You've already said that."

"—families from three different chapels don't mix. I feel sorry for the Scousers coming 'ere, because they've got no bloody idea what they're letting themselves in for."

"That's right, that's right. Stick up for the Scousers, not us. It's our town, they're not wanted. It'll change everything, and I don't want Winsford to change."

"It 'as to, it's been divided for too long. Anyway, the change can't be stopped now. Lots of families 'ave already moved in. Maybe it'll 'elp the town.

"Oh yes, and 'ow do you see that 'appening? By taking away fields and overcrowding schools. Don't talk daft."

Again the same put-down. I slammed my hand on the table. "I'm not daft," I shouted, "and don't look down on me as if I don't know what I'm talking about when I say something. I'm not daft and I'm not stupid."

My eyes must have been glaring because your mum looked away. When she looked back I could see in her eyes that she was sorry.

"I didn't mean that, Sam."

"Well, don't say it then."

"It doesn't mean anything, I—"

"It does to me, and it 'urts."

I should have left it at that and accepted her apology. I didn't.
"Ye're too quick to judge and put down."
Now it was her turn.
"No!" *her voice rose,* "no, don't you dare say it's just me. You were the one who believed the old bitch and took your belt off to Joe. You judged, not me, and now you're paying for it because 'e won't tell you about school, will 'e? Well damn well ask 'im, that's all it will take. Ask 'im."
"I'm not."
"Why? Because you're stubborn, is that why?"
"If 'e wants me to know, 'e'll tell me."
"What? 'E's dying to tell you. All you 'ave to do is ask 'im once and 'e won't stop. 'E's full of it. Every night when 'e comes in. Even with all the 'omework. 'E loves it."
I poured a cup of tea, my hand trembling, and I turned my back to her so that she wouldn't see my eyes begin to water.
"You know all that anyway."
Her voice was softer. "That's why the Sunday School thing came up, didn't it? You are right, I know, really. Sam, everything's changing in our lives — the town, the chapel, me and you, Joe, and Rose will eventually. We both make mistakes, and we'll make more. But as long as they're not too bad we'll get by. Ask Joe about school, 'e'll tell you."
"No."
"Then come with me to the open night next week and see for yourself. It's nearly half term and they go into streamed classes after Christmas. Come with me."
"No, I'm not."
"For God's sake, Sam, why not? Why won't you see ow 'e's doing?"
"I'm just not and that's it."
"Well at least tell 'im that 'e doesn't 'ave to go to Sunday School any more if 'e doesn't want to. Show 'im you're taking some interest."
I said nothing. Instead I walked past her and out into the yard. I'd had enough of talking.

At eight o'clock that night there was a knock on the door and the door opened. In walked Aunty Joan and Uncle Thomas.

"Coming in," Aunty Joan shouted through the kitchen/back-kitchen. Lassie jumped up, barked, and pushed open the middle door to meet them "'Ello, Lassie, 'ello girl. Who's a good dog then? Thomas, 'ave you got that lamb bone from yesterday?"

Uncle Thomas took it from the inside pocket of his overcoat, unwrapped the newspaper, and held the bone over Lassie's nose.

"Sit!" She sat. "Good girl."

"Go on then, don't keep 'er waiting," said Aunty Joan.

He didn't and Lassie rushed outside with the bone. Uncle Thomas closed the back door and they came through the middle door into the living room/kitchen. We were all sitting there watching the telly. "Hellos" went round the room.

"Move up, you two, and let your Aunty Joan and Uncle Thomas sit down," mum said.

We did. Aunty Joan sat, but Uncle Thomas stood.

"Is something up?" mum asked, "you don't normally call round after chapel." She looked up at Thomas. "Go on, sit down."

"We've got some news and then we've got to tell others, so I'll stay standing."

"Are you 'aving a baby, Aunty Joan?" I asked.

"Joe, shut up!" Mum said, red-faced. Dad threw a quietening look.

"Well," I offered, "you always said she wanted one."

I saw the flop hand twitch and I shut up.

Aunty Joan touched my hand. "Joe, I would 'ave loved a baby and thanks for asking. But I'm too old now."

"Oh," was all I could manage. Mum still glared. Dad and Rose watched the telly.

"The news is about the chapel," Aunty Joan said.

"Sam, turn the telly off," Mum ordered.

"But Mum, I'm watching it," Rose dared to say.

"Shut up."

The telly went off.

"It's going to be sold," Aunty Joan continued.

"Who's told you that?" my mum said, laughing. I laughed as well, but my dad's face was still, just like Uncle Thomas's.

"Sam?" she said, the smile slowly fading from her face as she realised it wasn't a joke. My dad turned to Aunty Joan who had started to cry, Uncle Thomas put his hand on her shoulder and lowered his head.

"What's 'appened, Thomas?" my dad asked. My mum had started to cry, she didn't need to hear.

"We had a meeting tonight in the vestry. Four of the elders from each of the three chapels were there. They wouldn't listen, Sam, it makes no sense."

"I'll bet it was the Prims," my mum said.

"Let 'im tell us. Go on, Thomas."

"It's right that Prims will be knocked down when the road is widened, and we all know it won't be for another five years or more, but plans have to be made and decisions are needed now. The area council for the Methodist chapels left it to us to reach a decision, but they said that once it was made there could be no going back."

"And?"

"There were three options given to us. The first was that when the Prims was demolished, their congregation would come to Over chapel, along with the congregation of St Paul's chapel, which would be sold off. The second was that we would all go to St Paul's, and that Over chapel would be sold off. Mind you, that option was a non-starter from the beginning because St Paul's needs a lot of work on the roof and inside, so all their elders backed coming to Over chapel anyway."

"So it *was* the Primitives!" Mum said.

"Yes, Violet, it was. They wouldn't agree."

"What's the third option, Thomas?" my dad asked.

"Sell both Over and St Paul's chapels and build a new one," he said, shaking his head in disbelief.

"It's madness. What a waste of money. Which four wanted that?"

"You know them, the four who are always bowling on the Rec."

"But two of them must be pushing eighty. They'll never see a new chapel built. What does it matter to them? They'll never set foot in the door."

"That's right, and that's exactly what they want."

"It's not right, Thomas. It should be the younger families having a say, it's their chapel as well."

"I know, but they say they represent all the congregation."

"Like 'ell they do. It's what they want, more like," dad said.

"Your right there, but there's nothing more we can do. All they said was if they couldn't have their chapel, then we're not keeping ours. 'Build a new one,' were their parting words."

"Oh Joan, Over's a beautiful chapel. There's no need to build a new one," Mum said.

"I know, love, I know, but the decision's been made."

The two sisters cried together, then Rose joined in because she didn't like seeing Mum cry. Mum put her arm round her.

"Hey, Rose, don't you be crying as well. I'm only sad because I wanted to see you get married there like I did and your grandma did. Don't you get upset. It doesn't matter."

But I could see that it did. It was like part of her would be lost. I wondered if the others felt the same. Aunty Joan and Uncle Thomas certainly looked like they did. It was about ten minutes before they left and I watched them walk off down the path before switching off the backyard light. Back inside, Rose was cuddled up on Mum's knee and Dad was watching the telly again.

"Anyway, Joe, your dad's got something to tell you," mum said.

"I 'aven't."

"You 'ave."

"You tell 'im."

"Oh all right then," she said huffily. "You don't 'ave to go to Sunday School any more if you don't want to."

It was a shock. Was it a trick, I wondered

"You don't have to say that because of what's happened." Why on earth did I say that? "But if you're sure," I added quickly.

"Me and your dad 'ave talked it over," she said, glancing across at him. He didn't look. "It's your choice now because you 'ave so much 'omework from school anyway. And you 'ave Religious Instruction at school, so you're not missing out."

I looked at my dad, but there was no response, no look, no nod of the head or smile. He just watched the telly. I knew then it was my mum's idea.

"Great, thanks Mum. I'll still go sometimes," I said just to please her. Christmas, Easter and weddings would be enough.

"Will I still go, Mum?" Rose asked.

"Yes, you'll still go."

"Good, I like it."

Mum gave her an extra cuddle.

"Thank your dad as well, Joe."

I looked at him "Thanks Dad," I said quietly.

"Mmmm."

Chapter 6

*W*hat would have been so difficult? Why didn't I say something? Stupid. Daft. Oh yes, I was stupid and daft all right. For not opening my mouth when it mattered. Is it too late now? Is it? Tell me about school, Joe, tell me now. I'll listen, I promise I will. Was it as good as your mum told me it was? I did ask her you know, every day. I was really proud of you and I told all of my mates at the mine, well, those that listened anyway. They didn't all want to know, though. We'd all sit there at break time and talk about this and that and our families. Most of us had young children, and everyone wanted to say how well they were doing at sports and school, you know, except when it came to me and Carl. We listened, but when it was our turn, no-one wanted to listen about school. We could listen, but we couldn't talk. It was as if we would have been bragging. All we wanted to do was say about our sons, just like the others had. But our sons went to the Grammar School and the others didn't.*

Do you remember Carl's son, Paul? He was a couple of years older than you, good footballer, but he never really liked the school. He told his dad it was too strict, too many whacks for doing nothing. He couldn't wait to leave and get a job. Anyway, he used to keep an eye out for you, to see that you weren't picked on. Did he ever tell you? No, I suppose not.

I don't know what Paul was like, but his dad, Carl, was quick tempered. He once had one of your sports teachers up against the wall for whacking Paul. Richards I think the teacher's name was. Three whacks just because he forgot one of his football socks when they had a match on. Bullying sod. If it had been you I'd have done more than just threaten him. Still, I know you had a better time of it. I wish my school days had been like yours. I know your mum wished the same. She used to love telling me all about what you were doing and how you were enjoying it.

I felt my hand being squeezed. My head jerked back in panic. He was having another attack! My eyes focused quickly, he was still. False alarm, I must have been dozing off. His hand must just have twitched, because he looked very relaxed at the moment.

57

Sorry, luv, I didn't realise you were falling asleep. I bet you're tired, aren't you. Me, I feel wide awake, even though it is the middle of the night. It's odd, I can see all the stars through the window, and yet I know that my eyes are closed. Anyway, as I was saying, I know that you didn't have a hard time of it because your mum would have said. I used to feel envious of the way you would tell your mum the stories. I always used to hope that someday you would tell me something first. I should have asked, shouldn't I? Why didn't I? Children are only children for a short while, and they never come back. You never get a second chance to hear that funny story told with the zest of the young. Why tonight can I see things so clearly? Why couldn't it have happened when I was a young dad? Why be wise now when there is nothing I can do to have another chance? Oh, how sweet the taste of the words would be. I can hear me saying them now: "How was school today, Joe?"

Chapter 7

"**J**oe Harrison!" All the heads in the class turned to follow the board duster as it flew across the classroom toward my head. I dodged it easily because I had seen it being launched. "Don't you dare fall asleep in my class."

The wooden handle bounced off the wall, and the felt part hit Gaunt's shoulder, showering him with chalk dust. Eric Litton was our foul-tempered Maths teacher, and today he was having a bad time of things. He glared at me.

"What was the last thing I said, Harrison?"

The look was definitely a you'd-better-know-or-else look.

"'Don't you dare fall asleep in my class,' sir." I offered. The few sniggers round the classroom sealed my fate.

"All right, that's it. Out here now!"

The seat flipped up as I stood and went to the front of the class. He went to the cupboard, the slipper cupboard.

"When you're ready, Harrison!" he shouted without turning.

I faced the windows, bent over, and touched my toes. The three whacks with the black pump quickly followed.

"Right. Now sit down and pay attention."

The whacks stung, but my red face was due to embarrassment in front of the girls. Mr Litton's was pure bad temper.

Nige grinned as I walked to my seat. I curled my lip and raised my eyebrows, making sure that Litton couldn't see me, of course, and sat down. I felt a sharp jab in my back. I didn't turn because Litton was watching.

"I'll get you for that," Gaunt whispered, still knocking the dust off his blazer.

"Did you say something, Harrison?" Litton said.

"No, sir."

"Well who did then?"

Christ! What is the matter with the bastard today? And I don't know why Gaunt is making such a fuss about the chalk dust, because he always looks scruffy, like he needs a good wash.

"It sounded like it was from you."

"I didn't say anything, sir," I said.

"Right, well shut up. I don't want to hear another word from you otherwise you'll have detentions for the next two weeks."

"Up yours," I wrote quietly on my general workbook.

Gaunt prodded me twice more before the end of the class. He was one of the shits who came in on the Northwich bus who thought he was hard because he had a brother in the fifth form. The trouble was his brother was one of the school bullies with his own gang of zombies. If you got Gaunt, his brother and the zombies got you, it was as simple as that. Basically you had to fend him off without hitting him. Still, next year would be a good year. His brother wasn't going into the sixth form, and it would be open season on Gaunt the shit.

When the bell sounded for the end of the lesson, Litton was still twitchy so everyone filed out quietly. In the corridor Gaunt gave me a sneaky kick.

"In the playground after dinner," he tried to snarl. Nige bumped into him. "And you watch it as well, Weed."

"Oh save me, save me, mammy," Nige pleaded, dropping on one knee, hands waving like Al Jolson.

"The playground," Gaunt repeated, then walked off to the drama class, as if he hadn't been acting enough already.

"Hey, Joe, do you need the toilet before the next class? You've got time," Nige asked.

"What? No why?"

"Well, just in case you were shitting yourself," he laughed, nodding after Gaunt.

"Ah stuff him."

"Yeh."

"Hey, come on, can't be late for drama."

"*Won't* be late for drama, more like."

We walked fast, no running. Three whacks or a detention for running. And no short cuts up the girls' stairs — three whacks or a detention for that as well. Why? Mustn't look up girl's skirts. Why not? No answer was ever given. So we walked fast all along the second floor corridor to the boys stairs, up to the fifth, and back along the equivalent corridor so that we were directly three floors above the Maths room. The girls' stairs were immediately to the left of the classroom. Still, rules were rules. Knackered, we sat down. Only to stand when Miss Prior entered. Then we sat down, the girls relaxed and the boys sat to attention all through the lesson. God, was she sexy. Short skirt and tits. My groin used to ache after drama.

And that was how Mondays always started. Maths and drama. Someone always got whacked on Monday mornings by Litton, and Miss Prior always had the boys' full attention. But could I tell my mum that? Certainly not.

I thought of skipping the playground after dinner and going to the school library instead, so that I would avoid Gaunt and the plague of zombies. But when I was in the queue for the dining hall the message went round that Miss Prior was on dinner duty. Excellent! That meant that she would be on patrol later and we would be able to stare at her incredible legs, and other bits, for half an hour. Even the sixth formers went into the playground when she was on duty.

The queue for the dining hall went quiet when she walked down the corridor, but after she had gone through the double doors to check on the girls' first sitting the normal pushing and shoving took place, and no matter how far up the queue you were when it started, you could bet that all the upper school kids would have pushed you to the back by the time the doors opened. Me and Nige shrugged and waited. In a few years' time we would be at the front.

The doors opened inward and three lads from the lower sixth rushed forward.

"Stop now!" the voice bellowed. "What sort of example do you think you are setting?"

Miss Prior had been expected, not him. All of the boys went quiet, and I mean everyone.

"Well? I asked a question," the voice boomed again.

I couldn't see his face but I knew it was Mr O'Neil. I looked at Nige, but he didn't look back. Any movement from now on could earn you three whacks even if you were near the back because that sod sensed things. Short, fat, with thick red hair and bushy beard to match, he was not a pretty sight, and the word was that his whacks were the worst, courtesy of his weight-lifting days at university. He taught sixth form economics and was scruffy, with leather patched elbows and frayed shirts, preferring to spend his money restoring old cars.

"Well, I'll tell you what sort of example you're setting, shall I?"

Here it comes.

"It's the wrong sort."

Brilliant, just brilliant! If that had been an exam question the school would have had 100 percent pass rate. He was always so predictable, but he enjoyed himself.

"Phwaarrrt!"

Now that wasn't predictable. Which fool had dared to break wind, and Jesus, did it have to be so loud? Sniggers broke out, and lots of us had to close our eyes and chew on our lips to stop ourselves from laughing.

"Who was that?" O'Neil roared. He looked beyond the three sixth formers who were standing ramrod straight, down the queue beyond the double doors.

"You three to the staffroom. Now!" he ordered without even giving them another look. They walked swiftly down the corridor, eyes to the floor, not grinning, not raising their eyebrows, nothing. Just scared.

O'Neil strode slowly, purposefully, exaggeratedly after them, his metal heels clicking on the concrete floor.

"It was here, wasn't it?"

No-one said a thing.

"I know it was here because whilst the evidence may be invisible, it is still detectable, wouldn't you say so?" he asked to everyone and no-one.

"Who did it?" he asked again, very nicely, so polite as to make you sick, but so threatening in his calmness. "You, boy, was it you?"

"No sir, absolutely not, sir."

And that was it. The death sentence. He had to punish someone. "But you know who it was don't you?"

I peered round Nige to see who it was. Mistake! O'Neil's eyes were like a hawk with almost 360 degree vision.

"Don't move, otherwise I'll be up there to see you as well," O'Neil said without turning his head from his current prey. My bowel nearly voided itself.

"No sir, I don't know who it was," his prey answered.

O'Neil's eyes were merciless. "Pity, because I think you do. In fact, I think it was you, wasn't it?"

"No sir," panic in the voice, "it wasn't, sir."

"Well if it wasn't, then I'm sure the real culprit will own up to save you, just as you are purporting to cover for the guilty party."

The kid was doomed. Even if someone owned up now there was no escape, because all O'Neil would say is that he shouldn't have covered for the other person, therefore he should be punished, and the other person would be in for it for not owning up sooner. Judge, jury, and executioner at a kangaroo court.

"To the staffroom, now!"

The kid walked back down the queue, head bowed, with glassy eyes.

"Right. Gentlemen, you must be hungry, so slowly, single file, into the dining hall before the dinner is cold. Table heads go straight to the serving hatches and mind your manners."

We all filed in and went to our allotted tables. Eight to a table, two sixth formers who were the table heads, two first years, and four others. The table heads brought over the two trays of food from the serving hatches and then divided out the food. And guess what? That's right, their portions were always bigger than ours. Complain? No chance, unless you wanted a fist in the playground or be branded a sneak by the teachers. This is the way the system was, and always would be. That was what we had been told on our first day at our first meal in the dining hall.

"The system works and is fair," the headmaster had declared. "Anyone abusing it will be punished. Pupils who complain are weak. Here at the Winsford Verdin Grammar School we expect pupils to stand up for themselves in a manner becoming of young men. You have come here as children but you will leave as young adults who can fend for themselves. It is right that the eldest pupils collect the food and serve it at the tables because this is what will be expected when you become master of your own house and entertain guests. It is also right that the youngest should clear away after their elders and betters as a mark of respect. No one serves who has not in the past cleared away. Everyone's time will come. You *will* learn to have patience and respect, and you *will* eat like civilised people."

The headmaster had gazed everywhere, seemingly making eye contact with everyone in the hall, his black university gown adding a real demonic feel to his gaunt features and thin, jet black hair.

"Gentlemen, allow me to draw your attention to the four tables to the east."

His arm swept out horizontally and pointed dramatically. Every head turned.

"You will see that there are no chairs at said tables, only benches and stools. These are for the slovenly. Those who hunch their shoulders instead of sitting straight, those who put their elbows on the table whilst resting, those who do not use their cutlery correctly and insist on using the fork as ones does a shovel, and for those who fill their mouths to overflowing. Those are the tables for the social outcasts who will never feel at ease, nor should they, in fine restaurants. Those are the tables for those who will only ever take a lady out for a meal once, such will be the shame of said lady that word will no doubt get around about such dreadful manners. Yes, gentlemen, those are the tables which determine, above all, your social standing, because manners maketh man. I trust they will always remain empty as they are today. Now, enjoy your meal."

So far so good, I was now almost at the end of my second year at the school and I had not sat at the eastern tables. Neither had Nige. We looked across at the staff table. O'Neil and Miss Prior were sitting chatting. The creepy fat sod had carried her tray over for her and then returned for his own. How gentlemanly! But we were really just envious, every last one of us.

The best place to watch any goings on in the two large playgrounds was from the steps to the French hut. Unfortunately today all the places were taken by the sixth form boys. We had to make do with sitting on the lower wall between the buttresses of the 20 foot wall which kept us apart from the Secondary School next door. Still, from here we did have a good view of the main playground.

"Here she is," Andy nudged, making me slide off the curved blue edging bricks.

"Thanks a bundle," I said, quickly jumping back up and turning round, just in time to see her step out of the tunnel from the girls' stairs

All the girls carried on knocking their tennis balls to and fro, and a few idiots stayed with their cricket against the wall, but most of us watched as Miss Prior's patrol began in the warm summer breeze. She was a line walker, and like a Scalextric car we knew every turn she would make. First she walked the netball markings at the top end, semi-circle too, of course, then followed the wings to the other end, semi-circle, then out, disappearing round the history hut into the second playground, only to reappear and join the lower semi-circle a few minutes later. She did the circuit twice, so that anyone who missed part of it could come in and still see it all — a bit like going to the pictures really.

Today was a particularly good day because the hot June weather meant a mini skirt. She always wore high heels, and a short sleeved blouse with the top button undone. It would have been nicer if it had been tighter, but still, there were signs of stress at the sides of her bust. Wonderful, just wonderful. So wonderful, in fact, that I never noticed Gaunt sneaking up. He yanked my leg and pulled me off the wall.

"Now you're for it. All that chalk dust was your fault."

Nige and Andy jumped down.

"We can't see him, Joe," they both said.

"I'm going to have you, Harrison," he said with a double-handed push to my shoulders.

"How about now?" I bluffed, pushing him backwards and hoping he would be scared off.

"Go on, Joe, smack him one. His brother's not around," said Andy.

"I don't need my brother to deal with this chicken."

He pushed me again, back against the wall. I was scared now, not of him, but I couldn't get into a fight no matter what happened.

"Sod off," I managed to say.

"Go on, Joe, hit him now," Nige encouraged.

"Yeh, come on, hit me now," Gaunt taunted, sensing that I was frightened.

I shrugged and walked off.

"Chicken Winsford shit!"

I ignored him and carried on walking.

"And what are you looking at," I heard Gaunt say to Nige.

Smack! Gaunt's lip split.

"A bloody mess, now fuck off."

Nige ran to catch me up.

"What's the matter? Why walk off. He's nothing, smack the bastard. It'll only be worse if you don't."

"Sod off Nige, you don't understand."

"I understand you're scared."

"I'm not scared."

"Yes you are, but why? He's nothing. You could beat him."

"That's not the point. I'm not fighting."

"Then it'll get worse."

"Let it." I walked off.

"Idiot." Nige stopped walking.

"Fuck off."

I stayed at the far end of the second playground until the bell went for afternoon lessons. I watched everyone line up, then slowly file in. When the last of the snake of people disappeared, I ran toward the girls' entrance to sneak up their stairs. But as I was about to turn into the tunnel one of the sixth form prefects walked out into the bright sunshine. Instantly her blue knee-length summer dress was caught by the breeze and blown up before she could catch it. Before my very eyes were the first pair of suspenders I had ever seen in real life! The tan coloured stockings ended to show her firm thighs and the tiniest pair of pale blue knickers I could ever have imagined. Those were certainly not school regulation navy blue serge attire. In a second the stunning image was gone, even before my mouth had finished the "wow" it had begun. The look on my face must have said it all because she gave a brief smile.

"You shouldn't be using these stairs, you know. If you're caught it'll mean the whack."

"Believe me, today it would be worth it," was all I could say. "Thank you God, thank you!" kept running through my mind as I raced up the stairs to my next lesson.

Chapter 8

"Ha, ha, haaaa." Witch. I refused to look. If she said hello I'd say hello back, but not when she just cackled. "So 'ow was school today?"

Where was she? The voice was in the yard, but where? I closed the gate behind me, still looking.

"Well?"

"It was all right," I said to no-one, wondering where my mum was.

"Just all right?" And up she popped from behind the dustbin, ant powder in one hand and a trowel in the other. I jumped. I hadn't expected her to be there. Well, who would? The dustbin was in the top corner of the backyard by the coal shed in a space just big enough for the bin.

"You are weird, mother. Haven't you anything else to do with your time?"

"They need killing."

"Why?"

"Because they do, that's why."

"Okay," I accepted, not wanting to get into that kind of pantomime argument. "But even if they do, what on earth made you look behind the dustbin for them?"

"They were climbing onto the dustbin lid and I 'ate touching them."

I walked over to see.

"Look, there's a big nest, with flying ones. Look at the wings on them."

I bent down to look. She flicked my head with the trowel.

"What was that for?" I said, brushing the bits of soil from my hair.

"Well don't get your 'ead too close. They might fly up at you."

"What?" I said, laughing. "They must have about two pounds of ant powder on each wing. I'm surprised they can walk, let alone fly. Look at the poor things."

"They're not poor things. And anyway they'll be dead soon."

"I expect they will, but isn't the ant powder supposed to poison them, not crush them to death?"

"Oh, ha ha, very funny."

I moved away from the dustbin fast, a look of fear on my face.

"What, what?" my mum asked, quickly looking down.

"That one there!" I pointed.

She looked, worried, scared even.

"It's got a funny head."

She moved her feet away, stepping from behind the bin, then peering over the top. "No it 'asn't."

"Yes it has. I saw loads of them with funny heads once. They almost had faces. Ugly things."

"Where?" she asked, half-believing.

"On the 'Outer Limits'. They'd invaded Earth."

She gave me a silent, thunderous look.

"Don't you play me up."

"But you did believe for a minute, didn't you?" I grinned and backed away. "Admit it."

"No, I didn't." She was full of indignation at being caught out. "And anyway, I asked you 'ow school was today."

"And I said it was all right."

"I bet it was better than that. Come in and tell me everything that 'appened."

"Mum, I just want to sit down and do nothing. I've been at school all day and I don't want to have to say everything that happened every day when I come in."

"Why not? You did when you first went."

"I know I did, but I've been there nearly two years now and it's just not that different each day."

"Come in and tell me anyway."

"There's nothing to tell."

I was annoyed and it showed. Every day was the same — tell me, tell me, tell me. Things could never come out naturally, they always had to be recited sitting down. Talk about the Spanish Inquisition!

She followed me into the house, ant powder and trowel still at the ready.

"Sit down in the kitchen and tell me."

"Living room."

"Kitchen."

"Suit yourself."

I sat down in the living room/kitchen, striped blazer and school cap still on.

"What 'appened?"

"Nothing."

"Something must 'ave done. Tell me."

"It was an ordinary day."

"I bet something 'appened. I'll just sit and wait 'till you remember."

"Why?" I asked, almost pleading at the stupidity.

"Because I will. And your dad will want to know."

"No he won't."

"Yes, he will. Tell me."

There was no way out. What should I tell her? About the whacks in Maths? Miss Prior's tits. Or the stockings and suspenders?

"Nige had a fight."

"Again? I don't know why you like 'im. 'E's always in fights."

"He didn't start it."

"It doesn't matter." She was annoyed, fidgety. "Can't you make any better friends than 'im?

"I like him, he's funny."

"'E's always fighting."

"He sticks up for himself, that's all."

"There's no need to fight."

"You just don't like him."

"No, I don't. Make some nicer friends."

"Why don't you like him?"

"Because 'e fights."

"Is that all?"

"Of course it is."

"Really? Are you sure there's nothing else, like the fact that he's from Liverpool?"

"No."

"Really sure?"

"Yes, I'm really sure. And you'd better watch your lip. You're not too big for a flop in it. What other things 'appened at school?"

"Nothing."

"Yes they did."

Of course they did, but I had no intention of going through every little bit of what happened. I kept quiet.

"Why don't you want to tell me?"

"Mum, for God's sake shut up."

She stood up, over-the-top angry.

"Now you watch your tongue, otherwise there'll be soap on it. I'm only interested, that's all. But if you don't want to tell me then that's fine."

"It isn't telling though, is it? It's like I have to go through everything for you. Why?"

"Well if you don't want to."

We now had the hurt look. It was a real masterpiece, designed to make you feel guilty. She walked to the middle door, I said nothing, I'd seen it before.

"All right." She rotated, "If you're not going to tell me anything, you can go on the errand for your dad straight away."

I looked up, "What?"

"Yes, that's right," she said triumphantly, "you can go now. Don't get changed, get off now."

"Where to?"

"The pet shop."

"Now?"

"Yes, now!"

"But I want a drink and a sandwich. I'm starving."

"Well you'll 'ave to wait."

"If I'm going to the pet shop I'm getting changed."

"No you're not. Get your bike out and get going."

"You're doing this because I don't feel like telling stories."

"I'm not interested. Your dad 'as run out of mixed canary seed and sunflower seeds. 'E wants it today."

"No he doesn't. He won't be feeding his birds at half past ten at night when he knocks off because they'll all be roosting. He could get the seed tomorrow morning."

"Well 'e won't 'ave to because you're getting it now. Up!"

"But it's halfway down the High Street."

"I know where it is. And the sooner you go the sooner you'll be back." She walked into the kitchen.

I took my cap off and flirted it at the middle door.

"If that was your cap, you're in for it," her voice said in the distance.

"Bloody alien," I whispered. It was no use me complaining so I took the list and money from the sideboard and went out to the shed. Three bad-tempered bangs later my bike was out, I slammed the yard gate behind me and walked past the other cottages.

"Ha, ha, haaaa."

70

Shut up, Circe. I should have shouted it instead of thinking it. She wouldn't know who Circe was. I'll bet she's never even heard of *The Odyssey*. I rode down the path from the bank, not caring if Aggie saw me and shouted. Her backyard had a brick wall next to the path to the cottages and she always used to complain about me riding my bike on the path. Old sod. For revenge I used to pull the carpets off the wall. She was odd, she always had some carpet or other hanging over the wall ready for a beating. They must have been a really dusty family. Still, today there were no carpets, so that meant no Aggie.

I turned left at the bottom of the path and headed straight along the road to the High Street. I was right at the end of Well Street, just going to the middle of the road to turn right when the gang appeared out of Hughes shop. They still had on their black blazers with Secondary School badges on the top pockets.

"Grammar bastard," one shouted.

Oh no, the accent. Scousers as well!

"Hey, look at the pretty striped blazer," another called out.

I tried to turn quickly, but the first one grabbed my handlebars.

"Where do yeh think you're goin'?"

"Nowhere."

"'Ey, 'e's a fuckin' Woollyback as well!" The second one swung his fist and bubbled my lip before I could move my hands. By then all five were round me. One pulled my hair back as I felt a kick to my leg.

"Smack the Woollyback again." He did. This time it was my ear.

"Rip 'is jacket, get the pockets."

I struggled, but my legs were still either side of my bike, and I couldn't get off because they were pulling and tugging at it.

"Oi, you little buggers! Leave 'im alone."

"Fuck off, you old sheep shagger," was the only reply to the shop-keeper who had come out when he saw what was happening.

A wicked slap was his reply, right to the side of the kid's head. Two more were yanked away from me. The others backed off.

"Anyone else want a slap? Because that's what ye short of."

"My dad'll 'ave yeh for that, an' 'e'll do yeh shop window."

"Yeah, yeah, yeah. Sod off back 'ome. Ye not wanted 'ere, ye little runts."

They moved away.

"Are ye okay?" Mr Hughes, the shopkeeper, said to me.

"Yeah. Thanks."

"Ye lip's a bit swollen."

"It'll go. I'm all right."

"Sods took ye by surprise, didn't they?"

"A bit."

He ruffled my hair, but could see that I was almost crying.

"No damage done. Off ye go."

I looked up the High Street to see where the gang were. They had just turned up Moss Bank toward the Grange Estate.

"Where're ye going to?"

"The pet shop."

"Ye'll be all right then. They won't be down again."

I nodded, crossed the road and pedalled fast so that no-one could see my glassy eyes and swollen lip.

"'Ey, what 'ave I bloody well told ye about riding up this path?"

"Awr shut up Aggie." I tugged at the rug as I went past but didn't quite pull it off the wall.

"I'll see ye dad about ye."

"See him for all I care." I rode up the path, my tongue testing to see if the swelling on my lip had gone down. It hadn't.

"Ha, ha, haaaa."

I ignored her, went into our backyard and let my bike fall against the wash-house wall. Some of the whitewash scraped off. I couldn't care less. Head down, I went into the kitchen, put the bird seed and change on the table, and headed straight upstairs. On step eleven my mum appeared from the living room.

"Did you get it all?"

"Yes."

I didn't turn or look.

"Well, your tea will be ready soon," she said nicely, obviously wanting to forget about before.

"I'm not hungry."

"Yes you are, you said so."

"That was before and I'm not now."

"Don't be awkward, and stop sulking. The errand's done now. Get changed and come down for your tea."

"I just said I'm not hungry."

I was bad-tempered now but still not turning.

"What've you been doing?"

Now she was getting angry again.

"Turn round and look at me."

"No."

"Turn round and do as you're told."

I turned. Her face dropped

"Satisfied now!"

I went into my bedroom.

"'Ave you been fighting?" she shouted as she started up the stairs. I slammed the door shut. "You 'ave, 'aven't you? Well you'll be in for it when your dad finds out."

She tried to open the door but I leaned against it.

"Open the door."

"Why?"

"Because I say so."

"It's my bedroom and you're not coming in."

"Oh yes I am. Now open this door."

"Why won't you just leave me alone?"

Bang, bang, bang. "Open this door!"

I turned quickly, snatched the door open, and she almost fell in off balance. I stared at her. "There! Satisfied now?"

"Who've you been fighting with?"

"No-one."

"Oh yes, well 'ow did that 'appen?" she said accusingly, looking at my swollen lip.

"A gang of Scousers from the Secondary set on me outside Hughes' shop."

"Why?" Now she was upset, too.

"Because I had my Grammar School blazer on. Now, are you pleased you wouldn't let me get changed?"

"Did you give them one back?"

"*What?*" I asked incredulously.

"Did you 'it them back?"

"Didn't you listen? There was a gang of them. Five. I was lucky that old Hughesey came out of his shop and frightened them off."

"But didn't you 'it any of them?"

"No."

"But you should've 'it at least one of them."

I couldn't believe my ears.

"Well, you really take the biscuit. Only a few minutes ago you were storming up the stairs reading me the riot act about fighting, and what my dad would do if I had been in a fight, and now you're telling me off for not fighting! Which one do you want? You can't have it both ways."

My eyes were filling up with tears of humiliation at being hit and not fighting back, and tears of frustration at my mum.

"Well—" she tried.

"Well nothing. I know better than anyone what my dad will do if I get into a fight, so I don't need reminding by you."

I slammed the door in her face.

"And don't go telling anyone I was beaten up," I shouted, "just say I fell off my bike."

I then lay on my bed and cried for being a coward.

I didn't go downstairs all night. My sister said goodnight at the top of the stairs, but I didn't answer. Later I heard my dad come in from work. My mum quickly had his supper ready and they went into the living room. I needed the toilet so I quietly crept downstairs and went outside. On my way back I could hear them talking as I walked past the middle door at the bottom of the stairs.

"'Ow did 'e get on at school today?" my dad asked.

"Oh, 'e 'ad a good day. 'E enjoyed all the lessons and 'e especially likes Maths."

My jaw dropped in astonishment. I hated Maths.

"That's good. 'E'll need it when 'e's older."

"Yeah, I wonder what 'e'll do when 'e leaves. I wonder if 'e'll be a teacher."

The way my mum spoke made it sound like a noble cause, a bit like the search for the Holy Grail, like only a few could aspire to it. Sod teaching!

"Give 'im a chance, 'e's only just started there."

"Listen, it soon goes. 'E's nearly at the end of 'is second year. 'E'll be fourteen in August, you know."

"Of course I know."

"Time flies though."

"Yeah, but not that fast. So 'e 'ad a good day."

"Yeah."

She wasn't going to tell him!

"Except for when 'e went to the pet shop."

Yes she was!

"Why, what 'appened?"

"'E might not want me to say."

Well, it was too late for that, she'd have to tell him now, the daft woman.

"Yer not leavin' it like that. What 'appened?"

"Five lads from the Secondary set on 'im."

"Where?"

I could hear him put his plate down.

"At the end of Well Street."

"Why?"

"Because 'e's from the Grammar School and 'e still 'ad 'is striped blazer on."

"Where were they from?"

"Off the Ponderosa."

"Scousers?"

"Yeah."

"Is 'e 'urt?"

"Swollen lip."

"That all?"

"Dented pride."

"Why dented pride?"

No reply.

"Why?" he asked again.

"'E didn't fight back."

"Not one punch?"

"No."

"'E should've thumped one of them at least."

I felt the lump start to form in my throat.

"'E was frightened."

"Anybody would be against five, but you 'ave to stand up for yeself." He thought I was a coward as well.

"'E's frightened of getting into a fight because of what you might do."

"Oh yes!" The anger was evident in his voice. "Blame me. It's my fault, is it? It's my fault 'e won't stick up for 'imself. Well, ye're not doing that."

"What do you mean?"

"Ye're not layin' the blame at my feet."

"It's not a question of blaming anyone. It's just the way things are with 'im, but that's why 'e's frightened."

75

"It sounds like ye blamin' me."

"I'm not, Sam, I'm not. And don't raise your voice, I don't want 'im 'earing. He feels bad enough as it is."

"So 'e should. Not fighting back!"

I heard him tut, and I bet he was shaking his head.

"Sam, listen, you've got to listen. I said almost the same thing to 'im, and it backfired on me. Yet the things 'e said back to me were right."

"Such as?"

She told him.

"I've been thinking about it all night," she continued, "we can't tell 'im not to fight and then expect 'im to fight back."

"'E's got to stand up for 'imself, though."

"I know, but we've got a problem with the way 'e sees it. 'E's more frightened of you than taking a beating off anyone. It's in 'is mind that nothing will be that bad."

"Christ, ye make it sound like I beat 'im 'alf to death."

"No, I don't. It's just that 'e's built a picture of that night that's so vivid and frightening—"

"And ye know all that from tonight! Give over."

"It is, Sam. 'E was annoyed about having to tell me 'e didn't fight back, but there was more. It 'as to be that."

"Well I can't undo it. What's done is done."

"But you *can* do something about it, you can."

My ears pricked up, this would be good.

"You could teach 'im to box. You boxed in the navy, you've always been a good fighter. Teach 'im 'ow to box to defend 'imself, then 'e'll be safe." *Please do it* seemed to underline every word she said.

Nice one, mum. If my dad taught me how to box I'd be all right because he wouldn't say anything about it if I had to box my way out of trouble. Yeah! Go on, dad, say yes.

"No! Never!"

I sat down on the bottom stair as though I had been hit on the top of the head. Why not, dad, why not? But I didn't want to listen any more. I went to bed. The idea kept running through my mind as I lay there. It was a good idea of mum's. It'd be great if he did teach me to box. What if I asked him myself? I thought if I picked the right time maybe he'd say yes. Yeah, great. It would be good doing something with my dad again, and I wouldn't be frightened of fighting either! Yes, I decided I would ask him, and I'd make sure I persuaded him. I felt good about it now. I checked my swollen lip one last time and laughed to myself. Soon there would be no more bullying.

Chapter 9

I *never knew you'd been listening that night, Joe, but I'd always thought it was a strange coincidence that you'd asked me to teach you to box only a few days later. If only you'd stayed and listened a little longer then you would have known my reasons for saying no, and our talk wouldn't have ended so badly. I did care, Joe, I cared so much. Yet somehow the message never seemed to get across. I just never seemed to say the right thing when it counted most.*

"Oh, why not Sam? You could do it. You could turn things round for 'im."

"Yes, I could, but I'm not teaching 'im 'ow to box."

"Why? It worked for you."

"Did it? Did it really work? Because if it did I must say that I really didn't notice it. All it seemed to do was bring more fights my way. For every one I'd beat two more wanted a go. No, I'll not teach 'im to box. He'll 'ave to deal with 'is problems another way."

"Well, you bloody awkward sod! What sort of a dad are you? You gave 'im the problem over fighting, so you can take it away."

"I wondered 'ow long it would take before ye said it. We both knew it was coming, didn't we? But it changes nothing. Boxers are born, not made. They're nasty bastards even before they learn to box. Joe's not like that, it's not in 'is nature. Boxing, if anything, would spoil 'im, not save 'im. This time ye're wrong, Vi. This time I know what I'm talking about. 'E's keeping clear of it for 'is own good."

"Well, what'll we do? We've got to do something?"

"Why 'ave we?"

"Because 'e's still a boy, and 'e's ours, and I worry about 'im."

"What, and ye think I don't?"

"You act like you don't most of the time."

"Thanks. Thanks very much, Vi. That's just what I want to 'ear. But I tell ye what, yer running up the stairs shouting and banging on 'is bedroom door, demanding to come in, isn't going to 'elp. That just adds to the problem."

"I wanted to know what was wrong."

"And that was your way of finding out was it, by embarrassing 'im more? And another thing, that's 'is room. And if he doesn't want ye to come in, ye don't force yer way in. Ye acted just as bad as the

kids that 'it 'im."

"Did I 'ell! That's daft!"

"There ye go again. Daft, daft, daft! Well it's not bloody daft! Ye were guilty of bullying just as they were."

"Oh, I can't do right for doing wrong, can I?"

"And ye can stop feeling sorry for ye'self. That won't 'elp either."

"Well I think boxing will 'elp."

"Listen Vi, for one last time, 'e doesn't need boxing. If 'e's frightened of fighting, big deal. If that's all 'e 'as to cope with in 'is life, it won't be too bad, will it?"

"It's a big deal for 'im now."

"Maybe it is."

"It would be a big deal for you as well."

"Yes it would. And I would probably 'it out, but that's not the way I want Joe to be. He's brighter than I could ever 'ave dreamed of being, and 'e'll find different ways to deal with problems. 'E'll fight without 'is fists. Look, I might not know what to tell 'im to do, but I certainly know some of the things 'e shouldn't do."

"But I'm worried."

"I know ye are, and 'e loves you for it. And so do I. But don't pester 'im about it, or shout and demand to know. Give 'im a bit of space. That way 'e can deal with it in 'is own way. Ye know, I didn't knock the fighting out of 'im even though I thought I 'ad."

"What do you mean?"

"It was never there."

Chapter 10

The next day at school I told the tale of the bike crash and thick lip. Nobody questioned it, because nobody cared, except me. Besides, Nige was in a worse state than me after the zombies had got him at the bus stop the previous night. Anyway, I had more important things on my mind. I was waiting for the right opportunity to ask my dad about boxing. The sooner the better was what I wanted. The only trouble was that he was on two-ten all week, and that mean that he was in bed when I went to school, and at work when I got home, so I had to go a whole week without seeing him. And because he worked on a seven day rotation he might even be working at the weekend, overtime of course, but still working. I'd just have to wait it out and plan exactly what I was going to say.

After all the pluses and minuses of Monday, the rest of the week had been steady, almost boring. Still, it would be the summer holidays soon, and I was looking forward to the break, and all the days up at the open air swimming baths. The summers at the baths were getting better and better. The reason? More girls! That was the very big plus about the overspill moving in. Lots of the families had young girls. Of course, lots had boys as well, who weren't all particularly friendly as I'd found out this week. But as long as you didn't wander into their 'areas' or be unlucky enough to bump into a group by yourself, there wasn't much trouble. Which was really the way it had always been in Winsford.

The only downside was that the bigger Winsford grew, the less places you could go. The Ocean fishing hole and Knight's Grange farm were now off limits because the Ponderosa nearly stretched that far, and all the Scousers played on those fields and went fishing there now. Over Hall was getting the same as well, which was odd, because at first only nice houses were built nearby at Beeston Drive and The Loont, but then all the fields and hedges behind the Hall gardens were levelled. They were laying pipes and drains all along the back so I wasn't sure what was happening there.

Still, there was always the baths in the summer. They were open from May to September and although they were geographically up Wharton, it was a trouble free zone. Well, very little trouble, say perhaps the occasional disagreement, nothing of any importance.

Anyone could go there because no-one had ever claimed it as their territory. And the reason for this? Easy again — girls in bikinis and swimming costumes. It didn't matter if you were from Wharton, Over, or Scouseland, everyone went. Everyone that is, except the young Scouse lads. Which was great for us Woollybacks because we could look at their girls without having to watch ourselves. Strange that they didn't like the baths, they preferred the youth club or street corners.

Thursday of that week was particularly hot and all day I'd been thinking about having a cool swim straight after school. As soon as it was home time I took the short cut across Hickey's Hill and up the backs. The view from the Hill seemed to change every day now. The old I.C.I. playing fields were nearly gone, and the fields to the back of the High Street down to the Drumber were now being built on. That was where the new car-free town centre was being built. It was to be a pedestrian centre only. It sounded good, but no-one from up Wharton liked the idea of the new town centre being in Over. The complaints and protests had done nothing. The days were numbered for the shops and houses across from the schools. Poor old Jasper.

"Ha, ha, haaaa."

I refused to look. Did she sit there all day just to do that? If she didn't, how did she know when someone was coming? Perhaps she really was a witch. Spooky. Oh well, in we go, I hoped the inquisition didn't take long tonight because the baths were waiting.

"Hello, Mum."

"'Ello, Joe."

I walked into the living room and waited. Cap, blazer, shoes off, still nothing. I kept looking at the middle door expecting her to float into position and begin the questions. She didn't.

"What's for tea?"

"I don't know yet."

What! She didn't know? Normally it was ready for five o'clock, and I was warned not to go out *or else.*

"Oh, okay. I'll get some sandwiches later then. I want to go up for a swim. It's been so hot in school today."

"Okay."

Okay? Was that it? I stared at the door again. It was odd. Still, I decided not to spoil it. I stood up and started to loosen my tie, gazing out of the window and down the garden as I struggled with the bloody Windsor knot. Apparently they were the smartest knots to have, but I personally wished that my Uncle Thomas had never shown my mum how to tie the knot. As a young man I think Uncle Thomas had aspired to being like the Duke of Windsor, but the knot was as near as he got. And now, in his bid to immortalise the old Duke, as if his actions had not already assured immortality, my Uncle Thomas insisted on demonstrating to everyone how to tie the most uncomfortable knot in the world. It should have been called the mantelpiece knot, because it felt like your chin was resting on a shelf.

Then I saw him. My dad was in the chrysanthemums. What was he doing at home?

"Hey Mum, why is my dad at home?" I shouted in the direction of the kitchen.

"'E came 'ome early."

"Why?"

Then she appeared at the middle door.

"There was an accident at the mine."

My face dropped. I quickly turned to the window again.

"Don't worry, your dad's all right. He was 'it in the face by some falling rocks. Nothing bad, just cuts and bruises. Anyway, they've sent 'im 'ome for a few days' sick leave."

I rushed out, straight down the garden to see that she was telling the truth.

"Dad! You all right Dad?"

"Of course I am." He looked up. One eye was bruised and blackening quickly, he had a cut over his other eye, a lump on his forehead, and a split lip.

"Dad, are you sure? Your face looks a bit beaten up."

"No it doesn't," he snapped, which took me by surprise.

"Well, just a bit swollen then," I offered.

"Yeah well. It's a bit sore."

"I bet it is. I thought my lip was sore on Monday, but it was nothing like that. How did it happen?"

"I was roof scaling, me and Carl, when a loose piece fell and 'it me in the face. Carl was lucky, it missed 'im. But because I was at the front I caught it on my 'elmet and face."

"I would have thought the peak on the helmet would have saved your face more."

"Well it didn't."

Again that sharp reply.

"Did it hurt?"

"A bit. Made me dizzy more than anything."

As he spoke he kept turning his head away, not wanting me to see the marks.

"I'm glad you're all right Dad."

"Yeah, thanks. I should've been more careful."

Lassie was lying on the lawn so I went over and stroked her.

"And what's the matter with you, you lazy girl? Can't you be bothered to get up and walk to me. Too nice in the sun is it?"

She wagged her tail lazily and the silver whiskers caught the sunlight as she turned her head, enjoying the attention. I looked across at my dad again and I decided to ask him about boxing.

"No! Definitely not!"

"But—"

"No!" He turned away.

"But Dad, you're a good boxer, a good fighter. I want to be like you and not be scared."

"No, I said."

"I don't want to start fights, I just want to be able to look after myself. Like you've always done. Auntie Nettie told us you were never scared of anyone. I want to be like that."

"No!" This time he was really angry. Too angry for what I was asking.

"Why?" I shouted back. "Why is it always 'no' with you? Hey? Tell me. No to this, no to that. Why? Why is it so hard for you to do anything for me? Tell me."

He ignored my shouting, keeping his head turned away, tending to the bloody chrysanthemums.

"Leave the damn flowers alone and look at me."

He didn't, so I kicked off a beautiful yellow head. He turned so fast it scared me.

"Now ye just watch yer temper. There's no boxing for ye."

"But why? Why don't you want to help me? Don't you like me? Is that it? Is that why you don't have any time for me?"

"Now ye're being stupid. Of course I've got time for ye."

"Have you? When do you take an interest? You don't know me. You don't know what I like and what I don't like. You only know what my mum tells you. Just like school. In two years you've never been to an open night, not once. And not once have you asked me

about school. You just don't care. I don't know why, but you don't.
I wish I'd never asked about your accident because on Monday you
didn't bother to come and see me when you came in from work, did
you? It was just a split lip and it didn't matter. Well it did to me!"

I turned and walked up the path

"That's it," I shouted back, "I've finished trying."

Chapter 11

No, you're wrong Joe, I did see you. I came up into your room before I went to bed but you had fallen asleep. You looked so peaceful, and you even had a smile on your face despite the swollen lip. I would have loved to have knocked those lads' heads together for you, but you had dealt with it yourself. In your mind it had gone. I could tell from the way you were sleeping. But there was more to that day in the garden than you ever realised, and certainly more than I ever wanted you to know. You could never have picked a worse day in your life to have asked me to teach you how to box.

Perhaps, looking back, I hadn't been on my best form when I'd gone into work for the two-ten shift. For a few weeks I'd been under pressure to apply for a different job at the mine, both from my workmates and the supervisor. But in the end I'd decided it wasn't for me. You would have thought that once I'd made my mind up, that would have been that. But no. People just couldn't leave me alone. They seemed to be going on about it all the time. Not saying much, perhaps only a few words. Yet each one had to have their say, even in the changing room before we went down the shaft. And it irritated me.

"It was yours for the taking, ye soft bugger. All ye 'ad to do was put your name down and ye would've 'ad it," Carl said as he picked up his card to clock-on.

"I didn't want it."

"Well, ye soft, that's all I'm saying, bloody soft."

"Well, if that's all ye saying, ye can give it a rest then."

"I will."

"Good, then we'll all 'ave some peace."

"Bloody soft."

"That's it, carry on. Ye like an old woman, Carl, always 'aving ye last word."

"Well ye need shaking up, Sam. That's all I'm saying."

"Just bloody well clock-on, will ye, and get in that changing room so we can put our overalls on. Otherwise we'll be late for the cage."

"Soft."

"Carl, shut up, will ye!"

"Yeh, shut yer gob, Carl."

The voice came from behind the next set of lockers.

85

"And ye can fuck off for a start, ye loud mouth, Scouse bastard," Carl replied recognising the voice immediately.

"Eh lad, if yer want to give it a go, I'm ready."

"Ready? Ye've still got the afterbirth on ye face, son. Come back in few years."

"In a few years this'll be our town."

I checked my lamp and nudged Carl, *"Ignore it, it'll fall off ye shoe as ye walk away."*

"What did yeh say, bollocks?"

"Ye keep out of it, Sam, I'll deal with this tater 'ead."

"Tater 'ead! Who the fuck d'yeh think yeh calling tater 'ead?"

A half-dressed Kenny Neal walked round the lockers.

"Well, ye're all descended from the Irish, aren't ye? Isn't that what Liverpool is? A little Ireland?" Carl asked.

"Yeh can talk. At least it's better than coming from sheep."

"Listen ye little shit." Now Carl was losing it and he stepped closer to Kenny. *"Ye've only been working 'ere a few months, and I've 'ad enough of ye already."*

"Leave it, Carl, the siren's gone. We're on work's time," I said, pulling him back and clipping his battery to his belt. *"Come on, let's get the next cage and let it go."*

"That's it, let it go. Do what 'e says Carl, let it go. Back off. Run away. Just like Sam's doing. Aren't yeh Sam, running away? That foreman's job is mine because I've got the balls to apply. You 'aven't, 'ave yeh, Sam?"

"Fucking newcomers," Carl said, back turned to Kenny, and finally walking out.

I ignored the baiting, but it was hard work. We walked down the corridor to the shaft entrance and joined the others in the queue. The cage came up and the grills opened. We stepped in and moved up to leave room for any stragglers, but when we realised there was only one left to come, we spread out again.

"Cage full," I called out. The grills closed. Kenny was about ten feet away when the cage disappeared below floor level without him.

"You fuckin' Woollyback bastards," was heard fading into the distance as we dropped underground. In the pitch blackness the conversations continued. No-one put their light on, it wasn't necessary, we all knew where we were going. And at the bottom of the shaft the lighting was as good as any street at night. In fact, the roads in the salt mine were just like up top, except that there wasn't as much

traffic.

"Ye've let us down, Sam," Stan said in the darkness. A few others agreed with him, as I expected them to do. Our shift had been together for years and worked well together as a team. We were all good mates, and generally felt the same way about things. "Ye should've applied."

"Well, I didn't and that's that."

"It doesn't make sense." It was Carl again. "Now that Jim's retiring, the foreman's job was yours for the asking. Ye would've walked the interview and tests, and ye know all the kit back to front."

"And so do ye."

"I'll be retiring meself in four years, what do I want it for? Ye've got years left. And a young family. The extra money would've come in useful, ye can't deny that."

"I'm not denying anything, I just didn't want it."

"Well 'eaven 'elp us if that Scouse bastard gets the job."

"'E won't get it. 'E 'asn't been 'ere long enough to learn enough," Eddie said.

"'E bloody well thinks 'e 'as."

"Thinking won't get 'im the job," Eddie added.

"Then who will get it?" Ken asked.

"Probably Bob Cope off number two shift."

"For fuck's sake, not 'im," Carl said, "'e's about as much use as a wet rag when ye want to dry ye 'ands. Thanks for droppin' us in it, Sam."

I kept quiet, invisible in the darkness. I'd been through all of the arguments about applying. I knew it made sense and the money would be very useful, but deep down I knew I couldn't handle the paperwork.

"Yes, you could Sam. I know you could," Vi had said.

"No, I find it too 'ard and I make too many mistakes."

"But that would stop the more you got used to it. It would, you know. You deserve this job. Who else can take over any other position on the shift? Who is always called in for overtime when someone is off sick? They know you're a good, reliable worker. And even the bosses 'igher up want you to apply, you told me that."

"I know, I know, and at first I was going to. But now that I've seen all the paperwork, I can't."

"Yes you can. We've been through the forms together, and you know what to do. And if new ones are introduced I'll 'elp you."

"It's all well and good sayin' that—"

"I will, I will. You know I will."

"Yes I know ye will." I smiled at Vi and her look meant everything to me, she would do anything to help me. "But a time will come when I will 'ave to write out reports there and then. Like for an accident, for example, and then it would be out. And I couldn't cope with that."

"Who would know?"

"Who wouldn't, more like. Ye know what it's like at the mine. Everyone knows everything, even 'ow many pieces of toilet paper ye use."

"Sam!"

"Sorry luv, but ye know what I mean."

"But it isn't that bad."

"Not to ye maybe, because ye make more allowances for me. But to others, especially the bosses, my spelling mistakes would seem stupid."

"Well tell them what it is."

"Then I wouldn't get the job anyway."

"You're not going to get it if you don't apply, so what's the difference?"

"The difference is that nobody except me and you would know. That's the difference." This time she nodded, there was no disputing the fact, and also no disputing the pecking order and jibes which were part of everyday life at the mine, friends or not.

She held my hand as we sat on the sofa. It felt good and I needed her understanding because I was turning away a wage rise that would have helped us a lot.

"You know, " she said, "I don't think the errors are as frequent or as bad as you think they are."

"Maybe not, but I can't tell. When I write something it all looks correct. I seem to be blind to some words. I spell them wrong but they look right. I just don't recognise the errors. And it's the same when I'm reading. Sometimes it takes me ages to read a sentence because I can't work out the spelling of a word. For some reason some of the letters look mixed up and I can't work out what the word is. It's frustrating, and it was like that at school. I was put in the bottom class because they said I was slow. I wasn't. I knew *exactly what was what in my 'ead, I just 'ad problems with spelling. Look Vi, please don't go on at me over this. I don't want to apply. I don't want it getting out that I can't read and write very well. People just think that ye're stupid."*

"But you're not, and people wouldn't think that."

"Wouldn't they?" I looked straight into her eyes, and we both knew the truth. "Look, it's not just for me, think of Joe. 'E doesn't want people saying things about 'is dad, especially now 'e's at the Grammar School. 'E's got enough on 'is plate as it is. And I don't want 'im thinking that I'm thick either."

"He wouldn't."

"I don't want 'im to even get a sniff of the problem. Please, promise me it's a secret."

"Of course it is, but you know 'e wouldn't think of it that way at all."

"Maybe not, but I really don't want 'im to know. I've got my pride as well. That's the reason I don't go to open nights at the school. I don't want to let 'im down."

"'Ow could you? 'E'd be thrilled to bits that you'd gone."

"I can't take the chance that one of the teachers will give me a piece of Joe's work to read and I wouldn't be able to. That's 'ow I would let 'im down. If that 'appened it would be all round the staffroom. And from there it only takes one teacher with a loose tongue to let it out, and Joe would 'ave a big problem at school."

"No, Sam, you're wrong. Something like that wouldn't 'appen. Not at the Grammar School."

"You know, Vi, you really are innocent. Of course it could 'appen, but I know I can make sure it won't. I won't make things difficult for Joe, I love 'im too much."

"And I love you too, Sam." She kissed my cheek. "I think you're wrong, but wrong for all the right reasons." She put her arm round my neck and kissed me again.

"I love you, Vi."

In the pitch darkness of the lift shaft I smiled an invisible smile, thinking of our early night last night. Carl disturbed the memory.

"Kenny will be pissed off with ye for that, Sam."

"Let 'im be, 'e's just a mouth on legs," I replied.

"They all are."

"*Now then, Archie, ye'll 'ave to learn to live with them because it looks like they're 'ere to stay,*" *Wilf butted in.*

"*Hah! I doubt that. Some of 'em 'ave gone back already, and the sooner they all do the better it will be for us locals.*"

"*Ye're not a local, Archie. Ye're from Darnhall,*" *Carl said, raising laughs all round, "ye're almost a foreigner yourself."*

"*That's right, laugh ye daft buggers. But 'ave ye seen 'ow they're building at the back of Over 'All. That will be a bloody big estate when it's finished. Almost reaching our lane at Darnhall when it's finished. And that's only for more overspill folk. We used to be in the country, but we won't be then. The town's growing too big.*"

"*Oh, give over the pair of ye. They're not all bad. Bloody 'ell, we've got enough rough 'uns amongst ourselves anyway.*"

"*Ye're right there, Stan,*" *I agreed.*

"*I don't know,*" *Archie continued, "if ye ask me, there's too many coming all at once. Me and the wife are thinking of moving from Darnhall to Wettenhall. That extra four miles will make the world of difference. It'll get rough. You mark my words."*

"*It isn't just one estate, Archie, there's going to be three.*"

"*Are ye sure, Stan?*"

Well, that's what the wife said, and she works in the council offices up there. She should know."

"*Well, then we're definitely going to Wettenhall.*"

"*Keep our fingers crossed we don't get any more taken on down 'ere,*" *Bill said, " It's bad enough trying to tell what that soft bugger up top is saying most of the time. The way them Scousers talk is terrible. I 'ope my kids dunna pick any of it up at school."*

"*Christ, that's right. Some of 'em will be going to your kids' school, won't they.*"

"*Not just some of 'em, Archie, a bloody big chunk will be. We're right on the edge of Knight's Grange. I don't know what will 'appen. Maybe they'll be put in separate classes, or something like that.*"

"*Anyway, talking about that bugger up top—*"

"*Awr just ignore 'im,*" *I said, "'e'll settle down. 'E just wants to find 'is place in the pecking order."*

"*Well, we all know where that is, don't we, Sam,*" *Carl said, laughing.*

"*But I don't think 'e knows yet.*"

"*Knees!*"

The cage was slowing down.

"Yes, mother."

We all bent our knees.

"I'm only saying it for your own good. Ye were that busy talking. Anyway, I won't tell ye again."

"Oh, don't be moody, Stan, it's only a joke."

"Fuck ye."

"'E's got a cob-on now."

"What the fuck's that?" Archie asked.

"'Aven't ye 'eard. It's what the Scousers say when someone's annoyed."

"Is it? Well, if I 'ear it again ye can put two bob in the fucking swear box."

The cage slowed and jerked to a stop. The grills opened and we walked to the trucks that would take us to the rock face, our eyes squinting at the sudden change in lighting.

"Who's missing?" the driver asked.

"Kenny."

"Fucking typical. 'E'll 'ave to get the next one. I'll give 'im a warning for that."

Carl nudged me, "Kenny'll be at ye all shift for that."

"Well, at least it will be a change from ye going on about the bloody foreman's job."

"Ah well, there's still time for that. Five o'clock this afternoon is the deadline. We'll work on ye before then."

Archie groaned when we arrived at the rock face. "Bloody 'ell, 'ow much dynamite did they use at one o'clock? Look at that bloody lot we've got to shift."

"Oh stop complaining, it's only the same as every other day."

"Yeah, and it was a lot yesterday as well," Archie carried on.

"It's always the bloody same, ye daft sod. Same blast, same load, and the same moaning off you. Now get yourself out so we can get started. Stan, gave 'im a kick to move 'im on."

"Ye'll be on your arse if ye do that again."

"Come on, you two, get moving. Sam, 'ere a minute."

"What today, Jim?"

"Roof scaling with Carl, straight off before those soft sods start clearing up."

I turned to go for the scabber.

"'Ey, and another thing, Sam. Put ye name down for my job, I'm recommending ye. Ye'll get it, I know ye will. There's already been

talks about ye. But ye 'ave to apply."

"*I don't want to, Jim." I walked off.*

"You awkward bugger," he said to the back of my head.

"I know."

I took my scabber from its hiding place and went to the platform which would take us up to the roof. Carl was already waiting there.

"Hey you! Shit-'ead!" Kenny came running towards me from the later trucks. "Was it you who shouted 'cage full'?"

"No."

"Liar."

"Ignore 'im, Sam. We've got work to do."

"Let's go."

I reached to put the chain across.

"I'm fuckin' talkin' to yeh," Kenny shouted, grabbing my arm at the same time. Those near to us turned at the sound of shouting.

"It was yeh, wasn't it? Yeh said it."

"Yeah, I did. Now let go."

"I'd let go if I were you, Kenny," Carl warned.

"I don't need your advice, pal."

"Listen ye little shit, I'm not ye pal, and ye do need advice."

"Or what? What will toughie Sam do. Eh, Sam?"

"Let it go, Carl, just like before, let it go."

"An' what's with yeh anyway? Is yeh memory goin'? A minute ago yeh said it wasn't you, now yeh sayin' it is. There's no fuckin' wonder yeh not up for the foreman's job, yeh too fuckin' daft to remember anythin'."

"Is that right? I said no because ye asked if I'd shouted it. I didn't shout it, I said it. So when ye asked if I'd said it, I answered yes. Seems to me that ye're the thicko."

"'Ey! Are we 'aving this roof scaled or not?" Jim shouted over.

I snatched my hand from Kenny's grip and turned away.

"Let's go up, Carl."

Then I felt the heavy push in my back.

"Don't yeh turn yeh fuckin' back on me. I'm not finished with yeh."

"No, Sam, forget it," Carl said, looking straight into my eyes.

"Right Kenny! Over 'ere now." Jim shouted. "Carl, take that fucking platform up, will ye!"

My heart was pounding. Take it up quick, take it up. Too late, he pushed again.

"Oh, I see," Kenny carried on, "you're a different type of

Woollyback, you're one with a yellow stripe up yeh back. Hey," he shouted loud and slapped the back of my head, "a coward Woollyback!"

In that split second when the words left his mouth I let go of the scabber and spun round, my right fist coming up directly towards his chin.

"No!" Jim shouted as he saw me turn. Carl grabbed for my arm, but he was too slow. Kenny tried to move back, but his body was too close to mine after the slap to my head. He was too late. My fist connected and he went down like a rock fall.

"Oh, for fuck's sake, Sam! Oh Christ, Christ! Sam what 'ave ye done." Jim ran over shaking his head.

"'E asked for it, Jim," Carl said. "'E 'it Sam first."

"I fucking well know that. I saw what 'appened, but you know the rules as well as I do. Any fighting and you're automatically suspended for three days. No exceptions."

"Turn a blind eye. We will."

"Can't do it, Carl."

"Well, that's it for the foreman's job. It's over now!" Jim said to me.

"I said I didn't want it anyway."

My mistake, though, was taking my eyes off Kenny. First rule of fighting, don't lose sight of your attacker. Somehow he'd got up from the punch, and before I knew it he'd landed two hefty punches to my right eye and mouth. I crouched and covered my head while the shock subsided.

"For fuck's sake, 'old Kenny," Jim yelled, but by the time he'd made a move I was at him myself. I felt his nose crack with my second punch, but he surprised me again. He didn't go down, instead he snapped two jabs to my forehead, one of them splitting my eyebrow.

"Come on lads, 'elp us out," Carl shouted, "before these two kill each other."

Kenny made one more mistake. His first had been fighting me, the second was that he tried for a haymaker knockout. I stepped in easily with another uppercut, and this time I got all my body under it. His teeth smashed together, the cracking sound was sickening. This time he didn't get up. But I never took my eyes off him, not while they pulled me back, and not while they carried him to the trucks.

Jim was shaking his head. "I can't fucking believe this. Ye're like *kids at school, instead of grown men. Go on, Sam, get in the truck. Ye're suspended as well. Ye'll be told when the disciplinary 'earing will be." He turned. "Dave! Over 'ere. Ye're roof scaling with Carl. Let's get moving, we're behind now."*

Chapter 12

I never mentioned boxing again after that and it was weeks before I even spoke to my dad again. That summer was a good one, hot all the way through, and I went swimming most nights after school, and then in the summer holidays I was up at the baths nearly every day. In fact I can't really remember having much to do with him all summer long. Perhaps it was because I was mostly out and he was working shifts that we didn't see much of each other, but I can't remember being bothered about it either. At first I was mad at him, but then I suppose I resigned myself to the fact that he didn't care enough to help me out. Anyway apart from one minor incident up at the baths the summer was good. Mind you, I was a bit worried that my mum might have told him that I left all my clothes at the baths one afternoon after swimming the Flashes, but luckily she must have decided not to. I think she thought it would only have made things worse between us if he had to tell me off again. For me, it couldn't have been any worse.

"Ha, ha, ha!" The door opened wider so that she could have a better look.

"Satisfied?" I asked.

"Ye shouldn't be walking round like that. Ye should 'ave some clothes on," the witch said.

"I have got clothes on, they're called swimming trunks."

She slammed the door.

Well, how about that. I finally got her to close the door. Now, if I could just get to my bedroom without my mum seeing me....

"Stop there!"

"Damn." I looked. Where was she this time?

"And what do you think you're up to?"

She wasn't in the yard, I couldn't see her through the kitchen window. I turned round. Nowhere.

"And where are your clothes?"

The door to the outside toilet was closed, so even if she was there she wouldn't be able to see me. A quick glance to the dustbin. No.

"Up 'ere."

And then I saw her. Well, to be more exact, I saw her head. It was sticking out of the sloping window on the wash house roof. I assumed that her body was still attached, although out of sight.

"Mother, what on earth are you doing up there?"

"Never mind about me, I want to know about your clothes. Where are they?"

"At the baths."

Her face registered disbelief.

"Surely you've not walked 'ome like that? Oh God, what are people going to say. Which way did you walk 'ome?"

"What!"

"I want to know who might 'ave seen you. Oh, the shame of it. Did any of your teachers see you?"

"I don't believe this."

"They'll think you're off your 'ead."

"What? They'll think *I'm* mad? Look at you. What'll they think of you, more like."

"I'm cleaning the windows. We don't want people saying we've got dirty windows. And don't change the subject. I want to know why your clothes are still at the baths." Then it dawned on her, I could tell from the change in her face that she had realised what I must have done. "You've swam across the Flashes 'aven't ye? Admit it, you 'ave, aven't you?"

"Yes."

"What 'ave I told you about never doing that? People 'ave drowned doing that. The currents there are really strong."

"I didn't drown."

"I can see that, but you could 'ave."

"I didn't though."

"Stop answering back."

"I'm going to get some clothes on," I said, heading towards the door.

"Don't you dare move. Wait there 'till I get down these step ladders." She was out within seconds.

"You know, Mum, you can't see if that window is clean or not from here."

"Cheeky devil! It is clean, I've just done it."

"No, what I'm saying is that you can't see it from here, so why do it?"

"Because you can see it from inside the wash house."

"But no-one goes in there."

"I do."

"Not very often."

"That's not the point. And anyway you can see it from your bedroom window."

"Really? Well I promise I won't tell anyone the next time it's dirty."

"Get back to the point. Why are your clothes still up at the baths?"

"Why? Do you think I should have swam back for them?"

"Don't be funny. No, I don't."

"Well then, are you suggesting that I should have walked down Weaver Street, across the town bridge, and up Gravel Hill in my trunks?"

"No, I'm not."

"What then?"

She gave up.

"I'm going for them now, when I've got some other clothes on."

"You should 'ave more sense than to swim across there. Your dad never did, 'e 'ad more sense. Sometimes I wonder what they teach you at the Grammar School, because it can't be common sense."

"My dad never swam the Flashes because he never learned to swim."

"That's not the point."

"I think it is, Mum," and I went to find some more clothes.

"Clever clogs," I heard her say as she went back into the wash house.

I quickly threw some more clothes on and was out again, this time on my bike. My legs were tired after that long swim but I had to get there fast so I could watch the entrance and make sure Victoria's brother had left before I went inside to get my clothes. Why did everyone except me seem to have a big brother? It was a real pain at times, especially today. Things had been building to this all through the summer holiday between us, and then he had to appear.

"Look, she's there again, Joe. I tell you, you're in there. She hasn't taken her eyes off you all afternoon, and she isn't turning away when you're looking at her. It's a sure sign."

"And you know these things, do you Ian?"

"Well, if she was looking at me like that, I'd know."

And he probably would. Ian had had more girlfriends than any of my other mates put together. I suppose if anyone recognised the signs, it was him.

"But we've been staring at her all afternoon, she probably wonders what we're looking at."

"We're looking at her tits and she knows it." Ian frowned. "Sometimes you're too slow for your own good."

Well, who could blame us for staring at those two beauties, especially in that white bikini top. God, Victoria looked good! We were standing on the top stage of the diving platform, leaning against the back rail while everyone re-grouped. This time it was Tim's turn to be the target. When the rest of us were ready we went, fast as we could, one after another, jumping off the top stage and bombing Tim. While he was treading water we launched ourselves at him, seeing who could get the nearest without hitting him. We also tried to twist into funny shapes before finally closing up into a ball before hitting the water. It was a good way of showing off to the girls, but you had to be careful not to curl up too late.

No-one ever swam near to the diving stage, it was for bombing only, and only a few poofs ever dived in anyway. The real skill was in bombing, and the best place to watch the bombing was by the safety rail on the right-hand side of the pool. That was because you couldn't be splashed in that position. The left-hand side was a no-viewing zone because someone would always do a bombshell to the side, sending water over anyone watching. But the right side was safe. The reason? The springboard was in the way. There was a lane of water between the springboard and the side of the pool, but it was a hell of a jump from the top stage over the springboard. Not many people tried it, and after Ian's failed attempt the other day, I doubted if many would try it in the future. Anyway, that was where Victoria Towers was now standing, leaning back against the railings, sunning herself and displaying her full bikini top for all to see.

We showed off for all we were worth. Even Ian, whose left thigh was sporting the biggest bruise I had ever seen, was giving it his best. Three days ago Ian had tried a bombshell over the springboard. He hadn't made it. We'd had to pull him screaming from the water. We all thought he'd broken his leg after he hit the side of the solid plank that was the springboard. But he hadn't, and after two days in bed he was back again. I looked at the big purple bruise on his thigh, and then looked at Victoria. The temptation was too much. Just think how she would look dripping wet. I decided to have a go.

"Don't even give it another thought, Joe. You'll never make it. I didn't," Ian warned.

"You just didn't jump hard enough."

"It's too far. Only a few of the bigger lads can make it."

Was he right? Probably. But what if I did make it? Think of the status, and Victoria's wet bikini top.

When Martin was in position as the target, I held back to be the last to go. That way I could have a longer run diagonally across the top stage. One, two, three, four, five, they all went. Then I ran across and launched myself, eyes darting between the springboard and the white bikini top. I didn't twist, I just sat cross-legged in thin air, like a floating genie, or rather a rapidly descending genie. It was going to be close, very close, but I reckoned there was enough room.

Only when I was about five feet off the water did the people watching realise what I was doing. I grinned, missed the springboard, and hit the water, the bombshell perfect. The initial splash was deceptively small, but when the water rushed back together after I had gone under, it sent a large fountain of water up and over the watchers. Victoria was right in the middle of them with nowhere to run. Excellent!

When I surfaced I could hear the screams from the girls and the cheers from my mates in the water. Victoria was glistening wet and pointing at me.

"Ye're definitely for it now," she threatened.

"I look forward to it, will it be soon?"

I laughed. She was faking annoyance but I swam away to the steps in the middle of the same side of the pool, then purposely walked along the side to the deep end, directly between her and the water, testing to see what she would do.

She stood out, as ever, to block my way, arms outstretched as if to throw me in. I couldn't believe my luck! She was actually going to wrestle with me! I half-heartedly pushed her hands aside, then stepped round her, my feet on the edge of the pool. She took the bait and reached to push me. I let her catch my shoulder and then stood my ground making her push against me with all her weight. Then I stepped back into the pool, wrapping my arm round her waist as I did so. She screamed and held on as we both went under the water. I could feel her skin against mine, it was like electric shocks to me. But she didn't let go, even when we surfaced.

"Now I'm really going to get ye," she threatened, without a hint of anger in her voice.

I broke away and swam for the other side. Not too fast, just enough to keep ahead. I reached the steps at the deep end, climbed out, and was over the safety rails before I turned to see where she was — up the steps, between the rails and still in pursuit. I ran past the big spectators' stand, past the fountain, and toward the cafe. Instead of going inside I ran past the entrance and through the glass door at the side, following the flagged path round the back of the big stand. From here there was a beautiful view of the Flashes, with the long, steep banks covered in bushes and trees. It was very popular for picnics out here, but food was the last thing on my mind when I saw her appear through the glass door.

I ran from the flagged path over the grassy area, following one of the many narrow paths that ran between the trees and bushes down the bank to the water's edge. When I was out of sight of the main path I stopped and sat down, half hiding near one of the larger trees. The half of me that wasn't hiding was easily seen by Victoria, and she crept up on me and grabbed at my neck when I made a poor attempt to escape.

Within seconds we were kissing. I'm not sure who started it, it just happened. The first kiss lasted for ages, my arms holding her tight against me. I didn't want to stop the kiss in case another one didn't start, but I shouldn't have worried. Her knees began to bend and I followed her down on the grass, another kiss starting except that this time she lay on her back and guided my right hand to her bikini top. I couldn't believe it, it was really happening! Her bust was in my hand! She felt wonderful through the soft material and her kiss became harder as my hand softly caressed her. I slipped her strap off her shoulder and went back to her naked breast. I never gave a thought that anyone might be watching, and neither did she. Then my stomach nearly did a somersault. Her hand slid down the front of my trunks and she squeezed. I gasped for breath, ending the kiss, and she laughed at her power.

"Good is it?"

I nodded.

"Then why don't ye do the same to me."

I nodded again, anticipation striking me dumb, and my hand set out on its journey to the unknown, gently moving over her flat stomach in search of the next piece of soft white bikini. Gently my fingers eased the material away. Christ! I was almost there! She sighed. I kissed her again and my hand moved down.

"And what the fuck do ye think ye're doing?" the deep voice shouted. We both jerked our heads up to look.

"Oh God, it's my brother!"

There was no mistaking the panic in her voice. Less than fifteen feet away was serious trouble, it was written all over his face.

"Christ, you'd better run. Quick, I'll get in 'is way."

She stood up, bikini top hanging down.

"What 'ave I fucking told ye about going' all the way, ye little tart. Ye'll end up pregnant before ye're fifteen at this rate," he yelled at her.

I took off. He was nineteen and almost twice my size, with the muscles of a brickie. I didn't need another look at him to know he was serious. I was looking for the best way to run, it was no good going up the bank because he was at the fork in the path and could easily head me off. I ran down the slope.

"Ye can forget about getting away. I'll teach ye to paw at my sister," he shouted after me. "And ye go and get changed, ye're going 'ome when I've seen to 'im," he yelled at Victoria.

"Creep," she said.

"Whore," was the reply. He started down the path. "That's right coward, run to the water. But ye'll not get away."

He was right, I was at the end of the path now, two feet from the bank and the murky waters of the Flashes. He wasn't running, just striding, menacingly, and seemingly enjoying every minute of it.

"Have ye wet ye'self yet, kid? Soon be time for a beating."

There was only one thing to do. I was in my trunks and he was fully clothed. I went in the water and began to swim.

"Ye'll never make it, ye're not strong enough. I'll just sit 'ere and wait."

I stopped swimming and turned, treading water to keep afloat. He was sitting on the edge of the bank, laughing.

"Come on, ye might as well come back now and get it over and done with."

I turned to look across the Flashes. I could hardly see the other side in the bright sunlight. Shit! I'd never swam anything like this distance. I knew some of the kids regularly swam back and to for a dare, but it was over a quarter of a mile across the lake, and the currents caused by the river Weaver flowing through made it a dangerous swim. I looked at him again. Now he was lying back enjoying the sunshine, he definitely wasn't going anywhere. I chose the swim. I knew I couldn't beat her brother in a fight, but I might be able to manage the swim across. He laughed again when he saw me swim away.

"Ye'll never make it," he shouted one last time, "and even if ye do, I'll get ye another time."

My arms and legs were tense with fear, and my stomach was tight. Relax, relax, or you'll sink, I thought. I coughed on the horrible tasting water. I started to panic, gasping for breath.

"Go on, drown ye bastard," I heard in the distance.

Up yours! Just think of Victoria's tits, I said to myself. Imagine that the prize for swimming the Flashes is a feel of her tits, the only difference is that you've already had it. I kept going, spurred on by the memory of the moment. It helped. Who knows, maybe I would get another feel, but not if I drowned. I wanted another feel.

My legs throbbed from kicking and my arms felt like lead when I eventually felt the soft mud at the edge of Platt's Fields. I'd done it! I squelched through the mud and dragged myself onto the grass, chest heaving, finally lying flat out until I felt like I could stand again. Now all I had to do was walk home through the streets in my trunks and act normal. Still, they were a great pair of tits.

I suppose the only thing I never understood afterwards was her brother. I bumped into him on the town bridge a week later and my heart sank.

"Nice swim, mate, I never thought ye would make it."

"Uh, er thanks."

"A word of advice, though."

Here it comes! He bent to whisper in my ear. "Next time take 'er where nobody can see ye."

I stood back, surprised. He winked at me and then walked off. No more bother. Thank God for that!

No luv, thank me. I knew about your swim across the Flashes, not from your mum, but from work. Ian's dad, Stan, told us all. We were all having our sandwiches when it came out. You were the toast of the shift that day, your first swim across the Flashes.

"Well 'e's done better than ye ever did, Sam."

"'Ere, 'ere."

I just laughed along with them, I didn't mind a bit. When we'd been lads I was the only one of the gang who never swam the Flashes. But you'd done it, and I was really proud.

"It must 'ave been the thought of them tits keeping 'im going," Archie said, causing more laughter all round.

"Anyway, it's only natural taking a girl round the back if ye can get 'er there," Carl said.

"Of course it is, Stan agreed. "But ye'll 'ave to 'ave a word with that bloody brother of 'ers, Sam, 'e can't go round picking on young lads."

"Don't ye worry. Me and Carl are calling for a pint in the Red Lion tonight after work. 'E's there every Friday. I'll just explain one or two things to 'im. 'E'll understand."

"I bet 'e bloody well will. Just go easy on 'im, remember 'e's only just out of a kid 'imself."

"I'll be on me best behaviour," *I promised, saluting like a boy scout. We all laughed again, and I loved it. My lad had swam the Flashes!*

103

Chapter 13

The door was opened softly. Bright light from the corridor rushed into the room. The nurse followed, closed the door behind her, and waited while her eyes adjusted to the dimness of the room.

"It's all right, Mr Harrison, I've just come to check his breathing. We'll leave the lights dimmed so that your dad isn't disturbed too much."

I nodded and stifled a yawn.

"You look pretty tired yourself. I won't be a moment."

She moved to my dad, checking her patient as only a nurse can.

"I think we can take the nebuliser off, he seems to be very calm now."

The hissing and spluttering faded away, and she carefully removed the mask from his mouth and nose.

"There, that's better," she said instinctively, although I doubted very much that my dad felt any change.

Oh, I can, you know. I feel much better than an hour or so ago.

"See, his face looks much more relaxed. If you ask me he's just had a nice dream and it's taken the tension away. A bit like having a laugh with friends."

Thirty seconds later she was gone and without the sound of the nebuliser the room was quieter than ever. My eyelids felt like lead. I looked at my dad once more and decided I would snatch forty winks. It would be dawn in a couple of hours.

"Do you know...."

"Tut, tut, tut."

I was nearly at the end of my second Murray Mint (I was given two now that I was fourteen years old, I think it was part of my advanced training) when Aunty Joan broke the silence. Uncle Thomas's eyebrows nearly hit the ceiling and his tuts were particularly annoyed.

"Oh it's all right, 'e's nearly finished, 'aven't you, Joe?"

104

"Mmm."

"See, he hasn't."

"'E 'as nearly, so it doesn't matter." Aunty Joan was determined to speak. "Do you know you'll be 'aving Mr Mills for English this year?"

I crunched the last piece in surprise.

"See, I knew he hadn't finished."

"Quiet, Thomas."

"Humph!"

"How do you know that, we don't start back until tomorrow?" I asked.

"We 'ave our ways, 'aven't we, Thomas?" She gave him a conspiratorial smile, but he ignored her, enjoying his sulk about the break in the silence.

It was hard to believe, wasn't it? I was fourteen years old and every Sunday night I had to sit sucking Murray Mints. Why? Because it was bath night and I had to sit and acclimatise before I walked home. I wasn't sure what Aunty Joan thought we did at school after games and P.E. when we had exactly five minutes to shower, dress, and get to the next lesson. There was certainly no time to acclimatise then. I suppose really it was a way of keeping me there a bit longer, so that I would sit and talk, which was sort of defeated by the Murray Mint silence training. At a quarter to eight they came in from chapel, at eight o'clock I arrived, at half past eight I was bathed and dressed, two mints to a quarter to nine, fifteen minutes talking, and then home. They led orderly lives, and I was part of it for an hour each Sunday. Tonight Aunty Joan had broken the silence five minutes early.

"Are you sure? It wasn't on the timetables at the end of last term."

"Positive," she said, and Uncle Thomas nodded gravely, ending his sulk.

"Well, how do you know?"

"Ahhh," he said and touched the side of his nose.

Aunty Joan ignored the secrecy. "I've been speaking to 'im."

"Mr Mills? How do you know him?" Now this was a surprise.

"Never you mind," said Uncle Thomas.

"Don't be silly, Thomas."

"Oh," was all he said.

"Mr Mills started lodging next door with Mrs Hillstock," Aunty

Joan told me.

"Since when?" Surely this wasn't true. Mills was a sod. I'd never had him for a teacher, but everyone knew. He was one for fondling girls' thighs and being sarcastic with the boys, always wanting to put them down, almost as if he was showing off to the girls how superior he was. Perhaps he thought they would be more attracted to him and the grope factor would increase proportionately.

"Since the beginning of August. 'E seems a lovely man. 'E's not been to University, only teacher training college, but 'e seems very nice. I've told 'im all about you, 'aven't I, Thomas?"

"Yes, but he doesn't know much about roses."

"Well you wouldn't expect 'im to would you, 'e's only been out of college a couple of years. 'E's only twenty-three, you know. This is 'is first teaching post."

"Really. So what have you told him about me."

"Oh everything. You know."

Brilliant, absolutely brilliant. That means he's now got so much bloody artillery to fire at me when he wants to have a go. Aunty Joan and Uncle Thomas were smiling at each other benignly, like they'd just done me an enormous favour.

"You'll enjoy his class. We're sure you will, aren't we, Thomas?"

"Mmmm," he replied in a very satisfied way.

The first few weeks of the new term were uneventful, boring really, and definitely disappointing on the Victoria front. Not that there was anything disappointing about Victoria's front, it was just that we never got together again after that day at the baths. Pity, so close, so damn close! Now she needed older, more mature boys, which, considering the dipstick she was now seeing, suggested to me that she was losing it. Bloody hippies had a lot to answer for.

The uneventful term changed in the fourth week. That's when it started. Tuesday morning, the third lesson was English. Despite the fact that since I'd started at the Grammar School I'd made a conscious effort to pronounce my aitches, that was when I realised I had an accent, or rather I was made aware of it.

As usual Millsy came in full of himself, but that day he seemed worse than normal. I think perhaps that he now felt his droopy moustache was fully grown, and he was able to make a statement about his trendiness with his facial hair. He didn't seem to realise that we all thought the Beatles were now prats with their long hair and moustaches. But good luck to him, because he needed help with his image. The George Best flares he must have bought from the Grattan catalogue looked ridiculous. Far too tight, they only accentuated his upside down taper — big hips, little shoulders. And his wide tie with swirls, unrestrained by a tie-pin, had a life of its own, almost mesmeric. He began.

"Right, today you chosen few shall recite for me. And to make sure we have enough verses to go round, I have chosen 'The Rhyme of the Ancient Mariner', which extends to over twenty pages with approximately six verses per page."

This announcement was greeted by low groans from the male side of the class.

"Oh, come on, a few verses each won't hurt you, and it really is very good, you know. So who wrote the work?" One hand went up, but he was ecstatic, it showed in his face. "Yes, Jane?"

"Coleridge, sir?"

"Excellent! House point for that, Jane!"

The creepy bastard. He only did that because of her thighs. Watch, in a few minutes he'd be over by her desk, groping hand at the ready. Still, she was the captain of the third year hockey team, and her thighs were good. I suppose I was jealous.

"Yes, of course it was Samuel Taylor Coleridge. And now, who better to start with than Jane."

Yes, who better indeed!

"Yes sir—

'Twas an Ancient Mariner
And he stoppeth one of three.
By thy long grey beard and glittering eye,
Wherefore stoppest thou me?'"

"Next." Another verse was recited.

"Next." Another verse.

And so it went round the class, but without him calling all the time. After thirty-one verses we'd all had a turn, and he stopped Jane before she could have another go. It looked like a fatherly pat on the thigh telling her not to put herself out, but we all knew it was the prelude to a proper grope sometime later.

"So tell me, what has become apparent during this reading of Coleridge's wonderful work?"

"It's boring sir," Susan Yard said. We all laughed, some louder than others. In Millsy's class it was all right to laugh if a girl made a joke.

"Well that's a matter of opinion and, of course, we are all entitled to our own opinions." He left out *if you're a girl*. "But that's not what I'm getting at. Anyone?"

He threw the question out again. "No? Perhaps we're on the wrong track, forget the poem."

Puzzled faces all round.

"Yes, that's right, forget the poem and consider the readers. What was different?"

"The speed of reading, sir" Angela offered.

"Not quite."

"The emphasis on the words."

"Now that's nearer, Catherine. What about some offers from this side?"

He meant us, the boys. Nothing.

"No? Oh well, back to the girls. Any more offers? No?"

He turned to the blackboard and wrote in block capitals as he said it. "ACCENTS."

"Accents, of course," he repeated as he underlined the word. "What makes the difference between understanding and confusion in the spoken word? The answer, your accent."

He stood and smiled, or smirked, it was difficult to tell. They were very similar now that he had his new moustache.

"Let me give an example. Jane." Now there's a surprise!

"Would you say this word, please."

He wrote "cart" on the blackboard.

"Cart," she said, which sounded like "caught".

"Thank you."

And now the even bigger surprise.

"Harrison, would you now say it."

"Cart." It came out naturally, to sound like "caart."

"You see what I mean. Both are from mid-Cheshire, but the accents are remarkably different, wouldn't you say?"

The girls said yes, and so did the lads from Middlewich and Northwich. But the few of us from Winsford, including Nige, said nothing.

"Now, why are their accents different?"

He postured, looking around but not inviting replies.

"Well, to understand that we have to look at backgrounds. Jane, what does your father do for a living?"

"He's an accounts clerk, sir."

"And does your mother work?"

"Yes sir, she teaches primary school children."

"I see. Yes, that explains it. And you, Harrison, what does your father do?"

For what seemed a lifetime I just stared him straight in the face.

"Well, Harrison, we're all waiting."

He looked round the room for support, grinning at the girls through his silly moustache.

"Surely you know."

And the silly girls laughed.

It seemed like every pair of eyes were on me. "You already know, sir."

"Yes I know I do, but I want you to tell us. You're not embarrassed, are you?"

"No I'm not," I said defiantly, "I just thought that maybe you would like to say it."

His face turned bright red, the explosion was on its way.

"What did you say, boy? Just tell us what your father does for a living, and watch the tone in your voice."

"He's a miner at the rock salt mine."

"And your mother?"

"She doesn't work."

"Thank you. Now, that wasn't too difficult, was it?"

"I never thought it would be," I replied loudly.

"One more word and you'll be out here!"

I glared in response.

"So you see," he continued, "the accents of Jane and Harrison have been influenced by the social circles of their parents, and whilst each has been brought up in the beautiful Cheshire countryside they have very different accents which will clearly aid or compromise them in the future. By reading out loud our English classes can help to refine accents and help the individuals aspire to greater things. But not Jane's, of course," he smiled.

"Now, let's take two more examples." He wrote "birds" on the blackboard.

"Sarah."

"Sir!"

"And Smallwood."

Nige didn't reply.

"Sarah first, please."

"Birds."

"And Smallwood."

Nige simply stared at him.

"Smallwood?"

Nothing.

"Smallwood, I'm waiting."

"Yeh can wait all lesson, I'm not playin' this game."

No-one moved.

"What did you say, boy?" Mills shouted.

"You 'eard."

"Out here, now!"

"Why?"

"Do it boy, if you know what's good for you."

"Don't do it Nige," I said.

"What did you say Harrison?"

"You heard."

He was purple. "Out here as well! Come on, both of you! Now!" He slammed his hand on the desk for effect. We looked at each other and decided to get up.

"You two can touch your toes."

He took the pump from the window ledge, but we remained upright.

"I said touch your toes!"

We stood defiant.

"Very well, we shall see about this."

He reached out and caught both of us by the short hair at the temples, lifted slightly, and walked us to the door, our heads tilted sideways and upwards trying to relieve the stinging.

"Open the door, Adams," he shouted. Adams didn't move. "Open the door, boy, or you'll be coming with us as well."

He opened the door.

"Now we'll see what the headmaster has to say about you two."

He was triumphant as we exited the classroom.

We waited outside the headmaster's study as Mills explained the problem behind closed doors. Then the door opened. "In here."

My stomach turned over at the chilling command. Me and Nige looked at each other, tried to grin, and entered the crypt.

"Thank you, Mr Mills, that will be all."

"Widj" signalled for him to leave. William Ian David Jones was the Prince of Darkness, and we were now standing before him. But more importantly, he was standing in front of the large black orna mental fireplace, his legendary whippy cane within arm's reach. It wasn't a good sign. I tried not to look at the cane, frightened that even merely glancing at it would cause it to spring into his hand, ready for action. Instead I stared at the floor, searching for the secret entrance to the catacombs where Widj's coffin must lie.

"Look at me, boy!"

My blood stopped flowing.

"The behaviour of you two this morning has been an absolute disgrace and you will be punished. Does either of you have anything to say?"

"No, sir," I said.

"Yes, sir."

My eyes opened wide, and I turned to look at Nige.

"Stand still, boy!"

I froze. His eyes flashed back to Nige. "This had better be good."

"I don't think that we should be singled out because of our accents, or have our families compared."

"Really. And do you think that as well, boy?"

"Yes, sir," I replied.

"Good, because I happen to believe that myself, and I shall deal with Mr Mills regarding that matter."

We must have looked relieved. Too soon.

"However, before you begin to believe this incident ends there, it does not."

He turned for his cane. I swallowed hard.

"I will not stand for insolence in pupils at this school. Do you understand?"

He flexed the cane between both hands, as if to warm it up.

"You do not answer back under any circumstances. Discipline at this school is based on respect for teachers If that disappears the whole fabric of the school will break down. I shall now enforce that respect in a way you will not forget. You will each receive three strokes of the cane."

"Why? We have done nothing wrong," Nige said.

"Six strokes, or be expelled. And you will be first. Bend over."

Nige flinched under the stinging cane. When he stood up, tears were running down his face from the pain.

"Now you, boy," Widj's face was bright from the effort, "bend over."

A heart attack would go down nicely now, but he didn't have one. Each swish of the cane heralded the stinging pain, but I did not let it show. I refused to flinch, and prayed that my eyes didn't water too much. They didn't. After the sixth stroke I stood up and stared with cold eyes, eyes like Widj. He returned the cane lovingly to the top of the fireplace.

"Now, do you have anything to say?"

"Yes, sir."

This time it was Nige who looked with shock and horror.

"Really! And what would you like to say?"

"For your safety, and that of Mr Mills, I will not inform my dad of today's events."

Nige closed his eyes, while Widj's almost popped out of his head.

"How dare you, boy! Are you threatening me?"

"Sir, if I might finish. As Mr Mills explained in his class just now, my dad's 'social circle' as a miner at the rock salt mine have a different way of dealing with problems such as these."

"Be very careful, boy, you are on the verge of being expelled."

"If that be the case, sir, and I am expelled, then I would have to tell my dad. Expelled, or caned again, and I tell him!"

"Get out, boy, before you regret your words."

I turned, quickly opening the door.

"And you."

Nige followed me. The door slammed shut behind us. My heart was pounding. I was scared stiff, but it hadn't shown. Nige just stared.

"You're a fuckin' nutter. Crazy."

"You haven't met my dad, have you, Nige?"

"No, but if he's anything like you've just suggested, I don't want to. Would he really come down and sort him out?"

"Yes."

"How do you know? Is he always fighting?"

"No, I don't even know if he's ever been in a fight."

"And you just said all that! What if Widj had called your bluff?"

"It wasn't a bluff. I just know it's how he would react."

"Bollocks."

I grabbed Nige by the throat, my eyes were cold, like they had been with Widj.

"It's not bollocks, I know my dad would look after me like that."

"All right, all right," Nige said, clutching at my hand. And in that split second I saw he was scared. He thought I was about to hit him. I let go.

"Sorry."

"Forget it. He would come down, wouldn't he?"

"Yeah."

We grinned and walked stiffly back to the classroom.

Chapter 14

Later that year there was a definite change in the mood of the town. The arrival of autumn reminded everyone that nothing lasts forever and the glorious summer days soon faded into memory, along with High Street which slowly but surely was being removed. For me, the old High Street died when they knocked down Jasper's shop. He had held out to the bitter end. I never got to sit on the sloping bench on school days. If only he could have lasted a couple more years, until I was a fifth former.

His shop stood alone for weeks, a silent reminder of the inevitability of change. Behind him the new shopping centre was almost ready, now he had to go. He was a reminder of the past that was no longer wanted, not in keeping with the new image of an expanding town. Even that was an understatement. Winsford wasn't expanding, it was exploding. And that was reported on the television, so it must have been true. Anyway, one morning Jasper's was there, and in the evening it wasn't. What chance for the rest of High Street? There was now a gap from the Rechabites Rest to Dene Drive, and now everyone knew, everyone who had ever hoped that this enormous change could perhaps be halted, were no longer in any doubt. It was now merely a matter of time. Someone had to take the blame for this, destroying a town with a history dating back to the Domesday Book — well, for Over at least. And the culprits were there for everyone to see and hear. The Scousers!

The three new council estates of Over, Glebe Green, and St John's were the worst ever built in the town. White boxes with flat roofs and no gardens. There was even a song released around that time about houses that looked like little boxes made of ticky-tacky that all looked the same; I would have sworn that whoever wrote that song must have visited Winsford.

Then they filled those little boxes with even more Scousers and Winsford couldn't cope. Everyone wanted their own way. Breaking old habits wasn't easy.

What I never understood or had explained to me was how changes like this came about. Did people vote for them? The answer to this had to be no. Were the changes to be made explained fully to the townspeople? Definitely not! Who pressed the green button and never said that there was a button coloured red which could be pressed if there was opposition?

I knew exactly which day Jasper's shop would be knocked down because it had been announced in the *Winsford Chronicle*. When I talked about it in my class, hardly anyone cared, and for the first time I realised just how few pupils from Winsford attended the school. Most of them caught the buses in to Winsford, and had never even been in Jasper's old shop.

After school only me and Nige sat on the chain at the cenotaph looking at the ruins of the shop. A Scouser and a Woollyback.

"Pity, that," I said.

"Yeh, I liked the old sod."

"Yeah, so did I."

"What d'yeh think of the new shopping centre?"

"Gruesome."

"Yeh, they're spoilin' Winsford. When we moved 'ere it was brilliant."

"Yeah, it was," I agreed.

"Are yeh walkin' up?"

"Yeah."

We didn't say much as we walked up the High Street until we were next to the police station.

"See yeh in the mornin'."

"Yeah, ten to nine at the cop shop."

"Right, see yeh."

I crossed over the road and walked along Well Street, and Nige went up to Moss Bank and onto the Grange Estate. I liked Nige, he was different. Most kids under the fifth year wore striped blazers, but Nige wore a black blazer. He said he didn't like the striped ones, but I thought they were great.

Mr Mills only ever had one more go at me, and that was when we were choosing our subjects to go into the fourth year. Those would be the subjects we would sit at "O" level. All of us were expected to take nine.

"Of course, you will not all pass nine. However if you do not try, you will not pass any." He smirked, and his moustache drooped lopsidedly. "I advise you all to choose wisely, because this choice will determine your life from now on, and will either open doors for

115

you or cause them to be slammed in your face. It is, of course, up to you."

Another smirk, some posturing, and off we went again.

"Some of you will no doubt have chosen already, knowing exactly the course you wish your life to take. Others will leave things to chance and, like a butterfly, will flit from this to that."

"I like butterflies," Nige said.

"We all do, but there are not many openings in life for butterflies, are there?"

Millsy looked to the girls for laughter and found it in abundance. Silly tarts!

"We shall, of course, advise you as to your individual choices as we see fit, taking into account both your aspirations and abilities. Of course, it would be wonderful were we all good enough to attend university. But alas, everyone is not equal, and some will have to make do with less."

"Did you make do with less, sir, or were you fortunate?"

Perhaps I shouldn't have said it, but the sweet taste of revenge was too tempting. He glared at me, and in that instant he knew that I knew. Good old Aunty Joan. The class waited for his studied reply.

"I was very fortunate, but it was due to a decision of my own making. You see, I had always known that I wanted to be a teacher."

"Really, sir?" It was creepy Jane with the thighs.

"Oh yes, even at junior school I knew that there was only one vocation for me, and I wanted to pursue that vocation with the utmost speed. With that overriding concern, I went to teacher training college for three years — that, of course, being the faster way to become a teacher."

"So is that better than going to university, sir?"

I recognised the voice of Angela Day, but I had to turn to look at her because the question was so stupid it deserved a filthy look. Thick or what?

"In my case, yes, it was, Angela. You see, it takes three years to obtain a university degree, and then you need to study for a further year to qualify as a teacher. In comparison, after three years at teacher training college you are already qualified to teach. It saves a full year."

He was proud of his explanation, you could see it in his face.

"But that way you don't have a degree, do you, sir?"

"No, Harrison, you don't. But that isn't the point I'm making, is it?"

"Won't it hold you back in the future, sir?"

"Why should it?"

He looked away from me, scanning the classroom, gauging reactions. It was an empty question, but his standing was now in question and he could not simply dismiss it out of hand. That would be to acquiesce.

"Well, I would have thought, sir," I was being painstakingly polite, "that if in the future you were to apply for other posts, then a qualified teacher with a university degree would seem to be better qualified than merely a qualified teacher."

"I would like to believe it wouldn't matter, and that a qualified teacher is a qualified teacher. Now, shall we move on."

"Sir?" I persisted, hand in the air.

"What?"

"Just one more question. Isn't it far more difficult to get into university than teacher training college?"

"No, I wouldn't say so. All further education is very competitive."

Smirk. Again he was very pleased with his answer.

"It's just that last week we were advised that if university was beyond us, we should consider teacher training colleges if we aspired to being teachers."

Game, set, and match.

"Who by?" The words nearly choked him.

"Mr Waverley, the careers advisor," I replied innocently.

"Well, Mr Waverley has been a teacher for nearly forty years and has very old-fashioned ideas. I can assure you that things are very different now than in his day." His face was definitely turning red. "Now, let us deal with core subjects."

I'd done it. I'd got him. The bastard had been blowing his own trumpet and I'd caught him out. So why didn't I feel good? What purpose had it served to alienate him even further from me? He was still the teacher and I was still the pupil. I also felt a little bit ashamed as well, but that disappeared in the next instant.

He turned back to me, his thoughts obviously collected. "Oh yes, before we deal with core subjects, perhaps Harrison would tell us what his aspirations are."

"To go to university, sir."

There were a few sniggers.

"No, no," he said to the class in partial admonishment. "Harrison is an optimist, aren't you Harrison?"

"I think so, sir."

"Oh no, definitely so. Otherwise you would never be here today. To aspire to be the first in your family to attend university is a challenge indeed, one which must be met with great fortitude and garnished with luck. Which of these two do you think you will be in need of the most, Harrison?"

"Perseverance."

He coughed a dismissive cough, turned to the blackboard, and began to write down a list of core subjects. Nige turned to me and shook his head, saying silently, no more, no more. He needn't have bothered, it was over anyway. Well, at least I thought it was, until later that day.

"Harrison!"

Millsy had been waiting. He must have seen me enter the toilets.

"I can't stop, sir, I'll be late for French."

"Then you will be late. I want a word about this morning."

He looked around before speaking further.

"Watch your fucking step, you little shit. If there are any more outbursts like this morning, I'll let everyone know that you live in house without a bathroom and that you have to call at your aunt's every Sunday night for a bath. How do you think that will go down? You'll be a laughing stock. Just remember, you're at this school because of a quirk in the education system, that's all. You can stop the pretence. You're getting above yourself, but I will bring you down as many pegs as is necessary. I don't like sneaks, and I don't like being bollocked by the headmaster because some urchin like you dares to complain."

"That was your fault."

"Be quiet when I am speaking, shit. You seem to have a chip on your shoulder a mile wide. Well, you will lose it here, I'll personally see to that."

"And what about yours?"

"Don't be insolent," he shouted, and raised his hand as if to slap me.

"You have no right to hit me," I challenged. "I'm not the one who infers they live on Swanlow Lane in their own large house, but you do. And just remember, you may know about me, but I also know about you. I know you lodge in the middle bedroom with the Hillstocks next to my auntie's. I know they insist you are in by 10.30 each evening and that baths are only allowed twice a week. You eat between six and seven each evening, anything she dishes up, and you are only allowed guests for two hours every Friday evening in the parlour. Now, is that really the lifestyle of a twenty-three year old out to impress the girls? Even Jane with the thighs will laugh at you when she hears. Playboy! Jack the Lad! No, just Millsy the Lodger."

"Harrison, I warn you, your mouth will be the downfall of you. Especially if this is repeated."

Even his moustache was quivering as he spoke.

"I'm not the one who started it, remember? What were you saying to me about having a bath? And don't worry about my dad coming to see you, I won't be telling him how you threatened me. I realise now that I don't need him to fight my battles, especially with people like you. You know, sir, the only difference between you and the school bullies is that you're older."

He was livid, but desperately trying to hold his temper. It had all gone wrong for him.

"Get to your class now!" he ordered.

"I'll explain why I was late, sir, shall I?"

"Move boy, and don't push your luck"

It was another hollow threat. I was getting better at calling bluffs.

"Run, boy!"

"Sorry, sir, I'm not allowed to. School rules!"

I smiled and walked away, leaving him glaring at the back of my head. Pity his next class.

Looking back I realised that the actions in my fourteenth year determined my life for a long time, too long in fact. It was a difficult age. "Aren't they all?" some parents might say. But for boys it is a year of momentous change, both physically and emotionally. Bodies seem to change by the week, day even, deep voice, facial hair, erections too numerous to mention, spots! And challenges. Every single day there seems to be another challenge. There was the pecking order, a ritual since time began, and that's just from the kids at the same school, let alone the kids from the Secondary.

Then the teachers are at it. Lording it over you. When you first start at the big school you are so small, innocent, and keen, and then slowly but surely they break you, either by sarcasm or discipline based on fear. There you are trying to cope with being neither a boy nor a man, and yet having to endure snobby teachers.

Who could I turn to? My mum didn't want to hear anything bad about the Grammar School, especially now that Rose was in the first year. Yes, mum was now in her element again, quizzing Rose on everything she did each day, and Rose complied because Rose loved it. From my dad there was nothing. He asked nothing and I volunteered nothing, and we grew further and further apart at a time when arguably I needed him the most.

I saw it, luv, I saw the changes. Saw them and ignored them, just like I'd been ignored when I was fourteen. My mam and dad made me leave school when I was fourteen then took all my wages as a labourer at the salt works, giving me only pocket money. I was nothing but another worker bringing money into the house. I felt rejected and it hurt, God how it hurt! So I shut myself off from them, put up a barrier to keep out the hurt. I blamed you for not telling me about your school. I thought you didn't want me to know, so as you left me out my barrier went up again so that I wouldn't feel left out. What I didn't see was the barrier you were building around yourself, not until it was too late. You had done exactly what I had done, how could I have let that happen? I should have been the one to help you, but how could I when I was the one who still needed help? I was too wrapped up in providing for the family with shiftwork and overtime that I ignored the other side of being a parent, where being approachable, listening, asking, are as important as anything else. Maybe it was for the best that I didn't know about the caning, because I probably would have been locked up for what I would have done. And then you would have had even more problems. And Rose.

I'd hated being fourteen, hated it. Everything had been so damn difficult. The schoolwork had become much harder as we started the "O" level syllabus. I'd had the run-in with Millsy and Widj, the Scousers were filling the estates behind Over Hall, I wasn't speaking to my dad, and then Lassie had died. When you grow up with a dog you know it will get old, but you still never expect it to die. I stopped being a boy the day Lassie died.

She'd stopped sitting at the top of the path on the bank a few weeks earlier, preferring to sit on her carpet by the back door ready to meet me when I came in from school. I'd known she wasn't too good because she had been losing weight and was moulting at the wrong time of the year. That day when I walked up the path I'd whistled and called her name so that she would have known I was coming. The door to Mrs Haspell's cottage had been open as usual, but there had been no laugh. Perhaps the witch had finally gone deaf, I'd thought

As always, as soon as I'd closed the yard gate I'd looked through the open back door. But there was no Lassie — odd! Where was she? Then I had seen there were no hairs on her carpet, it was clean. Slowly, I'd walked to the back door, each step heavier than the last, then I'd stood and stared at the carpet, knowing that she had gone. The tears had started immediately, but I'd made no sound. The pain of loss I'd felt in my chest had made me feel like screaming, but to who, and for what? No-one could have brought Lassie to me. So instead I'd gone quietly round the side of the house and out of sight. The wall had been my only support as I'd leaned back with my face up to the sky and cried for my dog. Lassie had entered my life when I had been one year old, I had grown up with her, and now she had gone. I'd stayed outside until the tears had finally stopped.

"You're late, Joe," my mum said as she took the bacon from the fridge.

"No I'm not, I've been outside. Lassie's gone, hasn't she?"

"Yes, love," and she started to cry, which started me off again. My mum put her arms round me. "She 'ad a good life, Joe, you mustn't be too upset." I heard voices from the living room, and looked toward the middle door. "Rose is upset as well, your dad's talking to 'er. Go on in."

"Yeah, okay." I brushed my eyes quickly, opened the middle door and walked in.

"And after French we go to the gym, but that's only on Mondays," Rose said.

"Oh, I see, and what about Tuesdays?" my dad asked her.

I froze, and my barrier was complete. He had never ever asked me a single question about school in three years and there he was asking Rose questions less than a month after she had started. I stared at him, a cold stare, and I felt the pain in my chest again as the tears began to rise. I ran out and up the stairs to my bedroom.

"Joe wait!" he called, but I ignored it and slammed the door. When they called me for my tea I pretended to be asleep. I wasn't hungry anyway, and I only went down for a drink when I heard Rose go to bed.

"Come and sit down for five minutes," Mum asked. So I did. The television was off, my dad sat there with his eyes closed, quietly crying.

"'E's really upset about Lassie, you know," my mum said.

"So am I."

I watched him cry and then went to bed.

Chapter 15

oe, you only saw part of it. Rose had been crying her eyes out as soon as she came in from school and we'd been trying to calm her down.

We were worried where you were because you were late getting home. All of us were upset, so I started to ask her about school so as to take her mind off Lassie. It worked for a while and that was when you walked in. I was going to do the same with you but you ran upstairs and wouldn't come down.

Me and your mum had decided we would all sit and talk about Lassie that night, remember all the funny times, no television. But you never came down. You didn't answer us.

"I'll go in and fetch 'im down," Vi said.

"No, 'e needs time to 'imself, let 'im alone. Give 'im 'is privacy."

"'E shouldn't be by 'imself, 'e should sit with us."

"'E'll come down when 'e's ready. Anyway, she's ready for bed."

"Yeah. Come on, Rose, up you go."

"Will Joe be all right, Mum?" Rose asked.

"Yes, 'e'll be all right."

Up till then I hadn't cried, because I knew it would only start Rose off again. When she'd gone to bed the thoughts of Lassie overcame me and I couldn't hold it in any more. I heard you come in and I knew that you were sitting watching me cry. Not a word from you, not a hand on my shoulder, nothing. Then I knew just how far we had grown apart, and I realised I was not only crying for Lassie but for you and me as well.

His hand gripped tight and my eyes shot open. He was gasping for breath. Christ! How long had he been like this? I pressed for the nurse and put my hand on his cheek, not knowing what else to do, trying to calm him.

She was there in seconds. "This isn't good," she said as she once more placed the mask over his nose and mouth, "not good at all. It's too soon after the last bout. He's fighting too much, hardly breathing. I'll have to give him an injection to calm him down."

"But won't that reduce his —"

"If I don't give him an injection he could have a heart attack very soon. Look at him, look at the stress his body is under. I don't know what on earth has triggered this off. Was he dreaming?"

"I don't know, I'm afraid I fell asleep," I replied guiltily.

She realised her tone had been sharp.

"Look, I'm sorry for that, but I must give him the injection."

I looked at the strain on his face as he fought for breath, the nebuliser hissing and spluttering, but this time useless.

"Go ahead."

The drug worked within seconds, combining with the nebuliser to steady his breathing. The crisis passed.

Chapter 16

My "O" levels were a disaster, both in the subjects I'd picked and the number I'd passed. Four, a grand total of four out of nine. Bad, oh, definitely. There was no bragging about the results at the chapel. Maths, English Language, French and Engineering Drawing. What a mixture, and not a science, not counting Maths, amongst them. Looking back I wondered what sort of careers advice I had been given about complementary choices, but I suppose I had been looked upon as one of those who should treat any "O" levels as a bonus, regardless of what they were in. Perhaps they thought I'd had some cunning plan conceived for my adult years where the mish-mash of choices would have some relevance, but really all I had done was pick the subjects I'd liked the most and yet still hadn't done very well.

In truth I wasn't surprised over the results, so there was no real point in being disappointed. And I couldn't blame my parents because they'd had no idea how to advise me anyway. I suppose I could have found a way to blame the careers master for the poor choice, but to what end? I'd failed the damn exams after all, and if I couldn't pass the subjects I liked, what chance would there have been with others? No, it was down to me, and the reports had predicted it. "Could do better", "Under-performing", "Unrealised potential", "Gets by when is capable of more". So what went wrong? Simple — I'd lost interest. The teachers were right, I'd done enough to scrape by, that had been all. Homework, basic then out. Projects, basic then out.

It took me two years to do "O" levels, and when I look back I don't remember very much about those two years. I'd stopped having any arguments with my dad because we hardly spoke, and I knew my mum stopped asking me questions about school because she'd been too busy quizzing Rose about her day. I'd had no real hobbies except making Aurora Monster Kits. I'd lost interest in sport at school because I'd been whacked by the sports teacher for grinning once while he was explaining how to jump a hurdle correctly. All told, I'd developed a real sod-it attitude. I suppose in my own way I'd been rebelling against the enforced discipline. It didn't help me to get on with the teachers, but I did it all the same. Summer nights and weekends were spent swimming, and winter nights out on the streets with some mates — only certain streets though. Bigger gangs had formed and had started to roam out of territory.

Nige always came down for me in the evening, never the other way round. Kids on the Grange Estate used to shout to get a reply so that they could check the accent. Woollybacks were fair game and in the end it wasn't worth the hassle of going into the Scousers' territory. But they wanted to go wherever they liked.

The big estates behind Over Hall were finished and fully stocked with new incomers. There they didn't even shout at you. If they didn't recognise you, they chased you, and I'm not even sure if Grange Estate Scousers were safe up there when the white ticky-tacky houses were first inhabited.

It was true that like will stick with like, or side with like, even if the 'like' was not at first apparent. Take Over and Wharton, the perennially divided villages of Winsford. They weren't 'like', but when the critical mass was reached regarding the Scousers, even the people of Over and Wharton sided together.

"We don't want any more bloody development, the town's big enough as it is."

That was my Aunty Peggy, one of my dad's sisters, talking. I don't know why, but she'd come to visit.

"Is she lost?" I asked my mum, who was just finishing drying the dishes.

"Shut up, don't let your dad 'ear you say that."

"She's never been before. I bet she had to ask directions, or somebody drew her a map of how to get over the town bridge."

"Shut it," she said, tea towel at the ready.

"I didn't think they could cross running water anyway."

"What on earth does that mean?"

"Witches, running water, you know."

"Now you'll get one in it in a minute if you carry on."

I turned and looked down at my mum.

"No I won't, those days of a flop in it are over. You have no right to hit me, you never had. But the difference is that now I'm big enough to stop you."

"It's the one thing that makes you listen."

"No it isn't. Its the very thing that stops me listening, but you never quite grasped that, did you? Just like the teachers at school.

They know what they are doing, and they enjoy it as well. It's all to do with power."

"Oh, shut up and stop going on."

"That's your answer all the time, isn't it? 'Shut up, you'll get one in minute', 'stop being moody', and the old favourite, 'that's that'. Every time you get stuck in an argument, or somebody makes a point you disagree with, you try to put them down or shut them up. Hasn't it ever occurred to you that you might be wrong sometimes?"

"Oh, I'm not talking to you when you're in one of these moods."

"Exactly."

"And don't you say anything in front of your Aunty Peggy."

"What, like 'What have you come for?'"

My mum scowled and walked out of the kitchen and into the living room. I followed. My dad and Aunty Peggy ignored us and carried on their conversation

"I tell ye, Sam, ye wouldn't believe 'ow they've built on them fields the other side of the railway line. There seems to be no end of it. There's factories and offices all the way from the Railway pub to the Bacon Factory."

"Well, it'll be good for the young 'uns. Plenty of work around and a lot more choice than we 'ad," my dad replied.

"More choice for the Scousers, ye mean. A lot of 'em are coming 'ere with jobs promised. They've already 'ad the interviews in Liverpool before they move. It isn't fair. What chance 'ave us, the locals got?"

"They won't take all the jobs, Peggy, don't be soft."

"I'm not being bloody soft. I tell ye, there's too many of 'em."

"From what I've 'eard that big computer place —"

"I.C.L."

"Yeh, I.C.L., and that canning company —"

"Metal Box."

"Metal Box," he frowned at being interrupted again, "will provide more jobs than there are young 'uns leaving school. It doesn't seem that bad to me."

"Ye've got yer bloody 'ead up ye arse, ye 'ave. I don't know who designed this growth in Winsford, this 'New Town' in all but name, but I tell ye this, they must 'ave their 'eads on backwards."

"Watch ye mouth, Peggy."

"Oh shut up and just look at it. The town's a bloody mess. We've got all the factories and offices, all the employment up Wharton, and ye've got all the estates up Over."

"So?"

"So! We've got one bloody small bridge over the river and everyone 'as to cross it to get to and from work. It's madness. Bad enough in the daytime, but in the morning and teatime it takes over three-quarters of an hour to get over the bridge."

My dad laughed.

"Oh, I see. It's bloody funny, is it?" Peggy said, shuffling on the settee.

"Well, I've 'eard it all now. Ye, of all people, complaining that ye can't get across the bridge to get to Over."

"It's not bloody funny. Ye've got the damn new shopping centre up your end. Where d'ye think we 'ave to shop?"

"Ye always 'ad to shop over the bridge."

"Yes but not that bloody far up High Street. Oh, yes, go on, bloody well laugh, ye ignorant bugger. It doesn't affect ye yet, but it will."

She shook her head, fidgeted, and sat back again on the settee. It seemed that every time she had a point to make she had to perch on the end of the cushion, stick her neck out, and point with her face, then sit back.

"Wait till your kids start work, and they're queuing up twice a day. It won't seem so bloody funny then."

"They might not work up there."

"Well, she might not," meaning Rose, " but 'e probably will," flicking her head to where I was sitting. "If what I 'ear about 'is 'O' levels is right."

"'E might be staying on, taking some again, while 'e does 'A' levels."

"Well then ye've got more money than sense. Get 'im out workin', that'll shake 'im up a bit. They 'ave it too soft these days. Our Greg's left, got a job already." She puffed up her chest and threw a cocky look at me.

"Seeing as 'e failed all three 'e took, it's not surprising, is it?" my dad said.

"Well 'e's got a bloody good job to go to anyhow. Sometimes it takes more than just brains." Another cocky look for me. "E's good with 'is 'ands."

"A monkey can peel a banana, but it can't make a fruit salad," I said.

"Ye cheeky little sod," Peggy erupted, almost coming off the edge of the settee. "Do ye always let 'im speak like this to 'is elders? 'E should show some respect."

"Then show some to 'im," my mum said. Nice one, Mum!

"Bloody 'ell, she speaks," sitting back again.

"All right, Peggy, that's enough. What 'ave ye come for?" my dad asked.

"Told you," I said to my mum.

"Quiet."

"Yes, ye shut up," Peggy barked.

"Shut up yourself," I said to her.

"Are ye going to give 'im one or shall I?" She was back on the edge of her cushion again.

"Hey, stop winding 'er up," my dad said to me. "Go on then, Peggy, I'm waiting."

"What for?"

"I want to know what ye've come for. Why the visit?"

"I've come for nothing. I just thought I'd pop round to see 'ow ye are. What's bloody well wrong in that?" She put on a hurt look.

"Knock it off, the last time ye called was when me dad died."

"All right, but when did ye last bloody visit us either?" The hurt look was replaced by a sneer.

"Ye all turned ye backs on me when I got married."

"Oh, ye're a funny bugger, Sam."

"Funny am I? Well I've got by so far without ye. So what do ye want, I've got me gardening to do, and I'm on shift at two. I'm not wasting all morning on ye."

"I'm ye bloody sister. Can't ye even spend five minutes with me?"

"Tell me when my birthday is."

"What the 'ell's that got to do with it?"

"Ye've never sent me a birthday card since I was married, 'ave ye?"

"Neither 'ave ye!"

"Liar!"

"Don't ye bloody well call me a liar, or I'll give ye a damn good slap."

"Try it any time ye like, but ye'll be wearing a sling when ye go 'ome if ye do."

This calmed her down a bit, perhaps because she knew that he meant it. But her tongue had its own way.

"That's it, ye 'aven't changed 'ave ye? It doesn't matter 'ow long ye live up 'ere, ye'll still always be a bad-tempered bastard from over the river."

I could hardly believe what I was hearing. Did she really want to be hit? How far was she going to goad him?

"Say what ye came for and leave."

"We want ye to 'ave me mam for a while."

Jesus Christ, no, I thought. There's no way in the world we want my gran living with us.

"She's not coming 'ere, and that's that!" Mum said. Now that was a surprise.

"I'm talking to the organ grinder, not the monkey," Peggy said dismissively with hardly a glance in my mum's direction. My mum's bottom jaw fell at the same time my dad's hairline nearly reached his eyebrows, such was his frown. I just sat there and waited, this was getting good.

"Watch ye bloody tongue, Peggy, there won't be a second warning."

I could see she believed him. She postured a bit and shuffled to the edge of the settee, just resting her bum on the edge. She leaned her elbow on her knee, her hand pointing. Her forehead was now just as creased as my dad's. They looked like twins. She had another go.

"And ye can knock it off as well. Ye might 'ave scared me once with that look, but since ye've been up 'ere ye've gone soft. All because of 'er." She flicked her head in the direction of my mum.

"Joe, out ye go," my mum said.

"No, I want to stay in."

"Do as yer bloody well told and get out," Aunty Peggy said.

"Shut up! I'm in my own house. You don't order me around."

She sprang up, faster than I'd expected her to be able to, her hand heading straight for the side of my face. But my dad moved quicker, caught her hand, and with his free hand grabbed her by the throat.

"Gone soft have I? Sit down," he shouted. Now she really was scared. She sat, trembling.

"And ye shut up," he said to me. "Sit and listen if ye must, but stay quiet."

I sat and listened.

"Yes, I bet ye've always been a nosy little bugger, 'aven't ye," Aunty Peggy said to me.

"Get said what ye've come to say, then get out," my mum now said.

"Don't ye bloody well 'urry me along, ye self-righteous cow."

"Peggy, so far all we've heard from ye is abuse. Why don't ye just go?"

"Because we can't cope with 'er anymore. She's wrecking the family. Argument after argument. And no-one else will 'ave 'er now. It's your turn."

"She's not coming 'ere," my mum said. "She rejected me when we got married, and underlined it when 'is dad died."

"My dad as well," Peggy added with tears in the corners of her eyes.

"Listen—" my dad started.

"I haven't finished yet, Sam," my mum interrupted him. "All ye lot left Sam out by 'imself, ye cut him off, and she was the cause of it. Well, you are welcome to 'er and the wicked tongue she 'as to offer."

"Bloody Methodists! There's not an ounce of Christianity in the lot of ye."

"Shut up and listen. She would 'ave only one aim if she came 'ere, and that would be to split us up. Well, it's not going to 'appen." Now it was my mum's turn to frown and point.

"Anyway, the cottage is too small. We 'aven't the room," my dad added.

"Even if we lived at the big 'ouse at Overdene there wouldn't be room. She's not coming."

"Is that it, Sam?" Peggy asked.

"I've told you 'ow it is."

My mum stood up. Peggy was about to leave.

"Well, ye are a bloody tough one, aren't ye? Are ye the same when 'e's not around?" she asked threateningly.

"I'll always be around," my dad said as he stood and put his arm around my mum's shoulders.

"Well, that's that then."

Peggy stood, her eyes glanced around the floor, then flashed at my mum. "There'll be no flowers on your grave from me."

That was the final straw. My dad grabbed her by the hair and walked her out of the house, across the backyard, and through the gate.

"Don't ever call again."

She didn't.

Chapter 17

ell, perhaps my family hadn't been the best example of like siding with like, but there was a general feeling of 'us' and 'them', and it had certainly manifested itself in the younger elements of the town.

My summer holidays, which had lasted all of July and August after "O" levels had finished, had been spent working up at the swimming baths where I had managed to get one of the cushiest jobs around, assistant lifeguard. How about that? I'd landed a job where I was paid to look at the girls in their costumes and bikinis! I certainly enjoyed that summer, even though I'd known that on the 26th of August, exam results day, I would have to come down to Earth.

It was during that summer, which again seemed long and hot, that there was a distinct increase in the number of fights in the town. They all seemed to be related to the movement of gangs into different areas. Most people could see the problem with fighting as it started to build and wondered where it would end. Looking back, I think everyone hoped it would fizzle out.

The Scousers still had their youth club near to Knights Grange, the Woollybacks had the swimming baths. At night time the shopping centre had become more of a lurking ground for Scousers in small gangs, and the town bridge area by the main post office was the Woollybacks'. Fighting between the Woollybacks from Wharton and Over had ended, and the Navigation pub, just along New Road and about two minutes walk from the town bridge, had an unwritten rule that sixteen-year-olds, Scousers excepted, could use the back room as long as they didn't get drunk or throw up.

Girls hadn't counted in this separation, of course, they had been more than welcome up at the baths and at the pub. I think that was what brought things to a head eventually. The Scousers hadn't liked 'their' girls with the Woollybacks, and they'd decided they would pay a Sunday afternoon visit to the baths, en masse. But word had got round quickly of the intended visit for that third Sunday in August.

The ringleader for the Scousers was twenty years old, had lived in the town for three years, and already had a criminal record from his Liverpool days. He'd been too old for the youth club by two years, but had hung around outside recruiting followers. It had been he who had looked upon the shopping centre as his night-time haunt, and he had gradually taken over the small gangs. From there he had decided he wanted the baths as well. In fact, he wanted the town, and he let everyone know it. His mistake was to let the word out about the baths visit one week early.

Woollybacks went to the baths in droves that Sunday, and when the Scousers crossed the town bridge and started up Gravel Hill they could hardly have dreamed of the reception waiting for them in Rilshaw Lane. Their gang of thirty or forty was hopelessly out-numbered as well over a hundred Woollybacks filed out of the baths and blocked the road. The looks on the faces of the Scousers said it all when the self-appointed leader of the baths mob shout-ed "Now!" All the studied cool and tough city images disappeared in the face of a hundred chanting Woollybacks. Common sense pre-vailed and the Scousers turned and ran, all the way back down Gravel Hill to the bridge, accompanied by the cheers of the gang who hadn't even bothered to give chase.

It should have ended there, but no, some people felt they just had to rub the Scousers' noses in it. The following Friday a gang of fifty Woollybacks went to the youth club unannounced and look-ing for trouble. It had been a tit for tat visit, and without the quick thinking of the Youth Leader the twenty or so Scousers in there would have been badly beaten up. While he had stood at the door delaying the Woollybacks' entry, his assistants had herded the Scousers out through a side door and over the playing fields to safety. He had then let all the Woollybacks into the club. They found no-one. Once again the situation had fizzled out, and should have died. It didn't because both sides always wanted the last word. Well, as far as I was concerned, the Scousers had it.

The next day, Saturday, at about a quarter to ten in the evening, six of us had been playing darts in the back room of the Navigation pub. I was standing at the bar with Kev. We'd just paid for the next round when the front door banged open and in burst Jill Mears, a regular Scouser bikini girl.

"Yeh'd better get movin'," she shouted out, her eyes wide and her breath in short gasps. "Fast! There's a gang of Scousers on its way up 'ere with pickaxe handles and bottles. They've just done two lads over by the bridge and they're looking for more."

"Out the back!" the barman ordered, "I'll 'ave no trouble in 'ere.

Go on, all of ye, out now. And ye," he looked at Jill, "out the way ye came."

I looked at Jill, about to say something.

"Get movin', they can't be more than thirty yards away," she screamed.

Kev was already shouting to the others as I turned to run down the narrow corridor leading to the outside toilets.

"Fuck 'em, we wouldn't 'ave run in our day," Albert said from his place at the domino table in the corner.

"Would we buggery," his seventy-year-old younger brother and playing partner added.

"Are ye knockin'?"

"'Old ye bloody 'orses, I'm thinking."

"'Ey, Ben," Albert called over to the bar. "While our Sidney's thinking about which domino 'e's going to play, if I were ye I'd go and get Bob and stand outside the front door, then them rough buggers can't come in. We don't want them spoiling the place."

"Good idea." Ben the barman always did what his dad, the landlord, told him to, and he followed us down the corridor.

We were already out of the back door and in the yard. The big gate was to the left but if we went through there we would be in full view of anyone on the road, and we could hear the gang now. They didn't sound like they were running but they were very close. The yard was surrounded by a six foot fence with barbed wire on the top. We were bloody well trapped! The only lucky thing was that 'Bastard Bob' the alsatian was in his pen, otherwise we would have been well and truly stuffed. The trouble was he was barking like a hound from hell. I heard a cry from the front of the pub.

"Shut up, listen. The dog's barking like mad at the back. Maybe they're getting out the back way. Split up!"

My insides almost melted at the shout and I ran at the fence, jumped, one foot hitting the railings half way up, and my hands grabbing for the top. Fuck the barbed wire. I managed a second step on the fence, then my arms straightened as I pulled myself up. Without stopping I swung my legs onto the barbed wire, ripped my new Levi's, and fell onto the grass on the other side. Four more bodies quickly followed, but Kev hadn't made it, he was too small to get enough height on the first jump. I heard him cursing, then we could hear a barrel rolling on the yard. It banged against the fence, then his head appeared.

"Don't fucking leave me!" he pleaded.

"Well stop pissing about and get over then."

He was over in a flash, and we ran to the right, away from the road and along the old railway track which had never had any lines there that I remembered.

"I can see the bastards!" Kev shouted. "Look! Down there by the big tree."

We didn't look, but the gang roared as it started to chase with renewed vigour. We ran straight through the gypsy camp which was always down there. It was normally a place to avoid, but tonight was definitely an exception. By the time the first caravan door opened we had passed through, but the Scousers hadn't. We then heard more shouting, but this time it didn't sound like teenagers, it was the sound of men. Very angry men.

"I'm going to 'ave to stop," Andy said, "I'll puke if I don't. That last pint's coming up."

"Puke and die, " I said, and kept running. He puked while he ran.

Up till now we had been running with the bank on our left and the bushes and trees on our right. Now we reached the bend where the trees disappeared and we would be exposed. We stopped and listened. Nothing behind us. Why not?

"Where the fuck 'ave they gone?" Kev asked, panicking, his head darting this way and that.

"I don't fucking know."

"Maybe the Gyppos turned them back," Kev offered in answer to his own question.

"What, all of them? Don't be stupid," Birdy said nastily.

"Watch ye mouth, shit for brains."

"Knock it off, you two," I hissed. "The last thing we need is a fight between ourselves."

From where we were now standing we could see the bend in the road. A car was coming along from the direction of the rock salt mine, its headlights following the snaking road by the river. The car horn sounded, and the fox hunt started again.

"Look, there the bastards are!" I pointed down to the road, and in that instant they saw us as well and started straight across the open ground toward us. There was a low rise to reach us, but it was steep, where a short embankment had once been built for the railway.

"Move it," Eddie shouted.

"Wait, it's too easy to follow us if we stick to the old line," I said.

"Well what then, smart arse?"

"We need to go up the bank and across the fields to Wades Lane Wood. We can lose them there."

"If we make it! I'll die before then," Pete said, "I can't run that far."

"You'll die if you don't. Now! Up the bank."

We scrambled for our lives, and at the top Pete collapsed, puking on all fours against the old tree. The full moon turned us into perfect silhouettes.

"Look, there they are," someone screamed, "there, up the bank by the tree."

More screams followed.

"Get up, Pete."

"Leave me, I've 'ad it. I'm finished."

Vomit and saliva dripped from his mouth as he heaved again. I looked at Eddie and he nodded. I grabbed one arm and he took the other, and we started to run, dragging Pete until he would run.

"All right, all right, ye fucking idiots, ye're scraping my best shoes. I'll run, for fuck's sake."

We ran. After another five minutes we were across the fields and on the edge of the wood. There we stopped running and lay down, motionless. We listened to the sounds of the night for what seemed like an eternity. The few shouts we heard seemed a long way off and we began to feel safer. We decided to move on and followed the stream as far as we dared. But we knew that we would have to break cover again soon because the wood stretched all the way to Grange Lane and the edge of the Grange Estate, which was exactly the wrong place to be. At some point the Scousers would realise that we had doubled back parallel with High Street.

I'd always known you had been down there that night. That's why I'd called in the Navigation after work. I'd been sitting in the front seat of Stan's car when he'd blown his horn at the gang in the road. Stan had kept his eyes on the gang, cursing at them, but I'd looked to where they were pointing. I remember it was a bright night, no clouds, and the moon was nearly full. I picked out a small group of people scrambling up the side of the bank by the old line. I strained to see who they were, but I couldn't see their faces, only their out-

lines. The first to the top had thick curly hair, and for a second I could have sworn it was you. It had set my pulse racing.

"Bloody 'ell, Stan, these mad buggers are chasing them up there. Look, can ye see, up on the bank," Carl said as he looked out from the back seat.

"'Ow can I bloody look? I've gotta be careful not to run these buggers over."

"What about ye, Sam, can ye see them?"

"Of course I can."

"There must be four or five of them. Christ, they'd better bloody run or they'll be in for it."

"There's six," I said. "Look, the last one's just reached the top of the bank."

Tommy laughed. "Well, look at that, 'e's on 'is 'ands and knees. Get up ye soft sod and run."

"Too much beer, I bet," Stan said, laughing with him.

"These young buggers aren't as fit as we were at that age."

"Bollocks, Tommy," I said, "I've never seen ye run in ye're life, let alone after a few pints."

"No, ye right, I've never ran. I would've stopped to fight. None of this running away shit."

"Give over, ye soft sod," said Carl. "This bloody gang's got bicycle chains and all sorts. Look there, that one's got a bloody pickaxe 'andle."

"Slow down, Stan," I said.

"What? Am I buggery! They'd knock my car to pieces."

"Then stop at the Navigation and we'll 'ave a pint. Let's find out what's going on."

Ben served us.

"'As 'e been in tonight?" I asked.

Ben didn't look me in the eye, he pretended he was concentrating on the head of the beer.

"Not seen 'im. 'E's usually down on Saturdays, but not tonight." He put the pint on the bar and looked away.

"What was all the commotion we've just seen?"

"Nothing I couldn't 'andle," he replied, again without looking at me.

"Bollocks," Stan said, "we've just seen a gang of thirty-odd chas-

ing half a dozen. Are ye saying that you saw them off?"

"That's what I'm saying. Me and Bob saw to 'em. One look at Bob and they decided not to bother."

"Where 'ad the six been?" I asked.

"What?" Ben replied nervously.

"The six they were chasing. Where 'ad they been?" He didn't answer.

"They'd been 'ere, Sam," Albert said from his seat at the dominoes table.

"But if that lot didn't come in, why did the six run?"

"Because Ben told them to," Albert added.

"What if they bloody catch them?" Stan asked.

"Well then they get caught," Ben said. "It's nothing to do with me. They must be after them for a reason, and I'm not 'avin my pub wrecked because of some kids."

"My pub," his dad shouted over.

I put my pint down. "I'll ask ye one more time, Ben, are ye sure 'e wasn't in?"

"Yes I'm sure," he said, lying through his back teeth.

"Because if I find out—"

"I'm not lying, I am sure." He licked his lips.

"'E's lying, Sam."

"Dad, for fuck's sake!"

My eyes blazed at him. "And all because ye didn't want ye're pub wrecked. I'll fucking wreck it myself after I've seen to ye," and I moved round the bar. Ben whistled, and I could see Bastard Bob bounding down the narrow corridor straight toward me. I watched the dog get closer and timed my kick to coincide with his jump. Thump! Perfect. His jaw snapped shut and his head jerked back from the force of my kick. The dog dropped and lay still.

"Now for ye, ye sneaky bastard." I dragged Ben from behind the bar, and pulled him down the corridor to the fenced yard.

"Give 'im a bloody good thumping," I heard his dad shout out, then laugh with his dominoes mates. Stan and Tommy blocked the entrance to the corridor behind me.

"Is this where ye let them run out to?" I shouted as my fist smacked his left eye, splitting the skin underneath. "Out to a yard with a fence so fucking 'igh ye can 'ardly get out?"

The second punch caught his right ear as he fell to his knees, arms wrapped round his head.

"Ye'd better pray that my lad's not been caught because I swear I will kill ye if 'e 'as." I kicked the snivelling bastard in the balls and watched him retch.

"That's enough, Sam." It was Stan.

I turned and walked to the yard gate.

"Now where are ye off to?"

"I'm going to see where 'e is."

"Are ye stupid? And what if ye run into that gang, what then?"

"Watch ye mouth, Stan."

"Christ, Sam, ye can't take 'em all on."

"Can't I?"

I went out of the yard and came back round the fence where you would have jumped over. I followed the old railway cutting, but I could hear nothing. I walked quietly, straining to hear a sound. Nothing. The gypsy caravans had their lights on and I started to walk past.

"And where might ye be going?" The accent wasn't local, or Scouser, perhaps a bit Irish.

"I'm going this way."

Three men appeared from round the sides of the caravans, each one had a heavy stick, as if expecting trouble.

"I don't think ye 'are, ye 'know," the same one said. "Ye see, I don't think ye should be walking into our camp without some sort of invitation, it isn't rightly polite."

He smiled, looked at the other two, then the look on his face changed to threatening. "So turn around and walk back the way ye came while ye are still able to walk."

"That stick will be 'alf way up yer arse in a minute if ye don't get out of my way. Now move and let me pass through."

"Oh, we certainly have a tough one tonight, don't we boys? Well it is an exciting night. First the small gang, then the large gang, and now the Lone Ranger."

He laughed, obviously pleased with his little joke. Then a door to one of the caravans opened. There was no click which meant that someone had the door ajar and had been listening. An old man with thick grey hair and a bushy moustache stepped out.

"The man looks serious to me, Dara. Step aside," he ordered.

"I will not."

"You'll do as yer father says," the old man flared, "now stand aside."

Dara moved, and his father looked at me. "My intuition tells me that yer son is in the first group."

I never took my eyes off the man called Dara for one second as I replied. "Seems like 'e was, and now I'm going to walk through 'ere and find 'im."

"So we are just going to let anyone walk through our camp, are we, da?

"Look him in the eyes, Dara, and tell me if ye see a man who is frightened. Because by God I tell you, I don't see one. Let him pass, we would be doing the same thing if it was one of us."

I walked past, eyes still on Dara.

"I hope ye don't find him," the old man said, "because it will mean that they found him first."

I started to run along the old track, then up the bank to the tree where I had seen the silhouettes. Nothing. I could see clearly, but there was no-one to be seen. And no sounds. Where would they have gone? I thought about where you would have made for, which part of the fields and woods you might know the best. Then I remembered that you used to go birds nesting in Wades Lane Wood, and that could take you behind the schools if you used it for cover. I decided to follow the stream through the wood.

"We have to cross the fields to the schools," I said.

"Fuck you, Joe. Bollocks to that."

"Then stay here all night. But if we go now we'll beat them to the High Street. It doesn't take a genius to work out what we've done, and sooner or later they'll realise. I want to get across before they appear."

"Listen," Birdy said. We froze. We could hear voices down the wood. "Oh shit! Some of them must have kept coming."

"Let's make a break now."

"Why not stay and fight," Pete said.

"Because we don't know how many there are, thicko."

"Ye'll be fucking answering to me in a minute, Joey boy."

"Save it, I'm off across the field."

I ran. I was followed by Eddie and Kev.

"Yellow bastard. And you two."

I'd been roughly level with Bakers Lane when I'd heard the voices.

I'd watched, motionless, as three young lads crept along one of the hedges. But I still couldn't make out their faces. I cut back through the woods, and headed for a point they'd have to pass. Again I watched from the seclusion of the bushes. Three lads passed by, no sticks, no Joe! From there I carried on up the woods until I reached Grange Lane, but saw nothing. Not even a sight or sound of anything resembling a gang. Everywhere was quiet, as though nothing had happened in the town that night.

At the High Street all was clear. There we'd split up and made our separate ways home. I'd run all the way until I'd reached the path up to the cottages. Slowly my breathing had returned to normal as I'd walked up the bank. It was only when I walked into the kitchen that I saw the state of my jeans and shoes, torn and muddy. When I looked in the mirror I saw that my face was flecked with mud just like my shirt. Quietly I'd taken off my shoes and crept up the stairs. I'd almost closed my bedroom door when the middle door downstairs opened. It was my mum.

"Everything all right?" she asked.

"Oh yeah, just tired, that's all," I said without turning round.

"Weren't you going to say goodnight?"

"I just didn't want to disturb you and dad if you were watching something on the telly."

"'E's not in from work yet, 'e's a bit late tonight."

"Oh. Well, anyway, goodnight Mum."

"Goodnight. Are you sure you're all right?"

"Of course I am. Goodnight."

"Goodnight then."

I'd walked up Grange Lane to High Street and then up to Well Street. Hardly anyone was around. If anything it had appeared too quiet. All the way I'd wondered where you might be. Were you at home, or lying somewhere in the fields beaten up and I'd not seen you? I felt sick when I finally reached home, sick because of what I might have found. But a feeling of relief had flooded over me when, through the opened door, I had seen your muddy shoes. I knew then that you had made it back.

"Sam, is that you?" Vi had shouted.

"Of course it is. Who else would it be," I answered, jokingly. The middle door opened.

"You're a bit late tonight."

"We stopped for a couple of pints."

"Well your supper's still in the oven."

"Right, thanks. Is 'e in?"

"Oh yeah, 'e's came in about thirty minutes ago. Went straight to bed, though. I think 'e must be overdoing it a bit with all this swimming every day."

"Did you see 'im?"

"Of course I did." Her expression was puzzled.

"And 'e looked all right?"

"Yeah, why? 'E was tired, that's all. Anything wrong?"

"No, no. It's just not like 'im to be early, that's all."

"Anyway, get your supper and bring it in, I want to finish watching this programme."

I left it at that, but before going in with my supper, I took your shoes and mine and put them outside in the wash house ready to clean them in the morning before your mum could see them.

Chapter 18

One week after my run from the Navigation I received my "O" level results, and one week after that I went back to school as a sixth former. Only it was no longer the Winsford Verdin Grammar School I attended, it had become the Winsford Verdin Comprehensive School. Yes, in 1970 Winsford became one of the first towns in the country to adopt the comprehensive system and boasted not one, but two comprehensive schools. The new Woodford Lodge Comprehensive School had been built behind the white ticky-tacky houses behind Over Hall, and the Grammar and Secondary Modern Schools had been merged to form the Verdin Comprehensive. Which school pupils attended depended upon where they lived in the town.

Our house, despite the fact that we were less than half a mile from the old Grammar and Secondary School buildings, and over a mile from Woodford Lodge, fell into the catchment area for the latter. For me that had made no difference because a sixth form had not been planned for Woodford Lodge immediately, but for Rose it was bad news. All her friends were in the catchment for the Verdin and, it had come as no real surprise, the Verdin had retained most of the old Grammar School teachers. So in actual fact, Winsford still had the same old regime in operation only under different names, for Verdin read Grammar, and Woodford Lodge read Secondary.

Of course, all officialdom denied that this was the case, but it existed all right, and our mum was having none of it. She'd decided that Rose would be going to the Verdin. Letters were sent to the headmaster of the Verdin, who, funnily enough, was Widj, Prince Of Darkness. But, flattered as he'd been, he'd said it was beyond his control. He'd advised writing to the Education Services in Chester, but they too had been unable to help. The matter was then brought to the attention of our M.P., who always had been, and no doubt always would be, Conservative. Perhaps it was because he'd firmly believed it to be foolish, or maybe he'd simply had nothing better to do, but anyway he'd decided to make an issue of the matter and had presented the facts to the Minister for Education, a nice lady called Margaret Thatcher. For her it had provided the perfect opportunity to make a token gesture against the Comprehensive system adopted and implemented by the Labour party, and although it had been too late for the Conservatives to do anything to reverse the plans for Comprehensive education in Britain, they could at least keep highlighting the failings of the system. And that was how it came about that my sister Rose was the subject of a letter from Mrs Thatcher saying that any child in Winsford had the right to choose which Comprehensive school they went to.

Big deal! The changeover was a shambles. The old Grammar School teachers hadn't known what had hit them when they began to teach ex-Secondary pupils. They did not have the fear factor any more and their "I say, you do" attitude was no longer effective. As for me, I couldn't have cared less. All summer long I had drifted into going back to school with my mum hoping beyond hope that I would eventually obtain the magical three "A" levels that would open the doors to University for her — sorry, I mean me. I'd known in the first week back that I wasn't going to stick two more years of school.

"'E's up to something Sam. There's three more letters for 'im today. Look!"

Vi held them out in her hand for me to see.

"And?"

"What do you mean, 'And?'?"

"I mean 'And?'"

"Well what does that mean?"

"It means 'so?'"

"So! Is that all you can say?"

"If Joe's got three letters, 'e's got three letters."

"Two of them are from companies. Look, their names are on them."

"So?"

"Stop that!" she shouted in frustration. "We've been through that game once already."

"Well, what if they 'ave got names on them? I don't see what the problem is."

"That's five letters this week already, and it's only Tuesday. I want to know what 'e's up to."

"And why must 'e be up to something?"

"Because 'e is, that's why."

"Don't be daft, they could be for a project at school. Information, that sort of thing."

"No they're not."

"Ow do ye know?"

"I just do."

"Ow?"

"Well for one thing they're too small to be information packs. They would be in a big brown envelope if they were. These are long, thin white ones. They've only got letters in them, I can tell."

"Maybe they're just answering questions. Now stop going on about it."

"I'm not stopping, I want to know what's in them."

"Hey, now pack it in. It doesn't concern ye, they're 'is letters."

"Yes it does concern me. While 'e lives in this 'ouse, it concerns me. And it concerns you, but you don't take any notice."

"Yes I do."

"When?"

"I do, and that's that!"

"Well I'm going to open them and see what they are."

"You are bloody well not."

"Don't you swear at me, I'm not your Peggy."

"No, but sometimes ye irritate like 'er though."

"Well thanks, thanks very much."

Now she put on her 'poor me' face. It lasted about two seconds.

"I'm opening them," and she went quickly into the back kitchen. I jumped up out of the armchair but by the time I'd caught up with her the first one was open.

"Well, I 'ope you know what you've just done."

"I've opened a letter, that's all," and she flipped open the folded paper and began to read.

"Ye stupid woman, ye've done far more than just open a letter. But ye can't see it, can ye? Give it to me," and I snatched it from her hand. She tried to grab it back, but I held it high so that she couldn't reach it.

"Give it to me, it's open now. I want to know what it says." Her voice was rising in anger.

"It isn't yours to read."

"Give it to me. I'm still 'is mother and I'll read it if I want to. Give it to me," she now shouted.

"All right then," I decided, "you read it, but don't ever say that I didn't try to stop ye. Don't ever blame me for what 'appens." I lowered my hand and let her snatch the letter away. She turned her back to me and started to read. I hung my head, I felt ashamed. "And don't tell me what it says, because I don't want to know." I walked out into the yard.

"Sam!" she shouted from the back kitchen.

"I don't want to know," I said quietly and without turning my head.

"Sam!" Her voice was clearer, she was standing at the back door, but she wasn't shouting anymore. Now there was disbelief in her voice. "'E's applying for jobs. Look, it's an invitation to an interview. 'E's leaving school."

"I said I didn't want to know."

"What do you mean, 'you don't want to know'? 'E's not going to do 'is "A" levels. It means that 'e won't go to University. I want 'im to go to University. Aren't you bothered? Don't you care?"

"Yes, I do care, and yes, I am bothered. But what concerns me more is what ye've just done and what 'e's going to say about it."

"What?" she said incredulously, "you're more concerned about me opening a letter than 'im leaving school? This is 'is future at stake, don't you understand?"

"I think it's ye that doesn't understand."

I walked off down the garden, shaking my head.

"That's right, walk off. Leave it to me to take an interest."

"Oh, ye've certainly taken an interest this time, all right!"

Maths, Geography, and Economics, what a pathetic combination of "A" levels! Who had I been trying to kid? There had never been much chance of me making it to University, but after one particular morning lecture with the bearded bastard I'd decided to give up trying. The first Economics homework essays had been returned after marking. It had then been time for the comments. All sixteen pupils in the class were mentioned, with each comment supposedly witty. It had been a wonder someone hadn't died laughing. Were we ever going to be allowed to grow up? I was seventeen for God's sake, and still expected to laugh at stupid schoolboy jokes that a twelve-year-old wouldn't have found amusing. Every comment had been a put-down of one form or another. The real joke was that sixth formers were supposed to be treated like young adults, yet the only sign of this was the concession that we could walk down to the chippy at dinnertime. Finney's steak pie, chips and gravy had become the highlight of the day, but that afternoon even they could not stop me thinking about the jobs I'd applied for.

So far I'd received two replies out of seven. One was a "Thanks for the interest, but no thanks," and the other had been an invitation to an interview in Altrincham with a company of chartered surveyors. It hardly seemed possible, but they had actually liked my meagre "O" levels because they contained English, Maths, and Engineering Drawing. It had been an encouraging start and I couldn't wait to get home and check the post.

"You did what? You opened my letters?"

I shouted in disbelief. "What on earth gives you the right to interfere in my life like this?"

"Oh, stop being dramatic, I only opened a letter."

"They're all open, all three of them!"

I couldn't believe it. I kept staring at the letters and then at my mum. "Is nothing private?"

"I'm your mother, and I wanted to know what you were up to."

"Oh you did, did you? So you decided to open my post and see for yourself?"

"Yes I did!"

"I am not a child!" I shouted, "and you do not have some God-given right to know the ins and outs of everything I do."

"While you're in this 'ouse I do."

"Really! And is my dad aware of this?" I gestured, holding up the opened letters.

"Yes 'e is."

"So he went along with it as well, did he?" She said nothing. "I'm surprised he took an interest."

"And that's all I was doing, taking an interest."

I stepped very close to her, bent my head, and put my face right in front of hers.

"No, you weren't, you were being *nosy*!" I shouted, making her jump in fright. "You were prying because you feel you should know everything. Well not any more! I'm sick of it, and the sooner I leave school and this house the better!"

I walked out of the living room and went upstairs to my bedroom.

"What does that mean?" I heard her shout from the bottom of the stairs, her tone now more inquisitive than challenging.

Twenty minutes later I had read the letters, changed from my school uniform, and was going out.

"And where do you think you're going? Your tea is almost ready."

"I'm going for a swim."

"No you're not."

"Yes, I am, and you're certainly not going to stop me."

"'Ave you any 'omework?"

"Yes."

"When's it got to be in by?"

"Tomorrow."

"Well then, you're not going until it's done."

"Stop me," I said in defiance.

"It'll 'ave to be done."

"No it won't."

"Don't be stupid, of course it will."

"No it won't. It doesn't matter any more because I'm leaving school."

She followed me into the backyard and watched as I got my racing bike out of the shed.

"You'll regret this when you get a detention for not 'anding it in."

"No I won't, because I won't go to the detention."

"Well I'll bet you do," she said, grinning, nodding her head like the perfect know-all. "You'll change your tune in a few days, when you've got out of this stupid mood over a few daft letters."

Every word, every new comment, had hardened my resolve to move away, let alone leave school. As I cycled down the path and pulled off one of Aggie's rugs, I became more and more attracted to the idea of the job in Altrincham. I really didn't know what commercial surveyors did, but it had to be more interesting than school.

There were hardly any people at the swimming baths that night, just a few swimming and a few sitting in the cafe. The evenings were cooler, and the coming weekend would be the last one of the season. After that the baths closed until May the following year. That night there was no-one bombing off the top stage so I tried swimming the day's irritations away. It didn't work, but Jill Mears provided the distraction I'd needed. She hadn't gone to swim, but had called in at the café with a couple of her friends toward the end of the evening.

When I saw her walk in I stopped swimming and rushed to get changed so as to catch her in the café before she left. My hair was still dripping wet when I thanked her for warning us in the Navigation a couple of weeks earlier. She'd smiled and I'd done my best to keep the conversation going. It resulted in my walking her home from the baths, trusty racing bike at my other side. The outcome? A date with her on the Saturday to the Palace cinema. So the day hadn't ended too badly after all, two interviews arranged and a date with Jill.

The Saturday film had turned out to be rubbish, so we'd left halfway through and spent the night walking round the town. Nowhere special, we'd just walked, talked, and held hands. Down Weaver Street, up High Street, down Grange Lane, up Nixon Drive (Scouseland), along Delamere Street and down to Moss Bank. We stopped on the corner.

"Yeh don't have to walk me up here."

"Why not? Don't you want to be seen with a Woollyback?"

"Ha, ha," she said sarcastically, "it's too late fer that, isn't it. After all the people we've seen out and about tonight."

"Yeah, you're right. Are you bothered?" I asked.

"No."

"Me neither." I looked straight at her. "So I'll walk you home then."

"It might not be a good idea, because yeh'll be walking back through the Grange Estate by yehself."

"But I'm safe with you, am I? You'll protect me if a naughty gang comes up to us, will you?" I said mockingly.

"No, I didn't mean that." She sort of laughed. "No-one will bother a couple, but by yehself, well... it's different."

"I'd be fair game, is that it?"

"Yeh, something like that."

"I still want to walk you home."

"Okay."

She shrugged, gave a big smile, and linked my arm, obviously pleased with my decision.

We'd arranged to meet at the swimming baths the next afternoon for the last day of the season, and after a goodnight kiss I'd started to walk back. And guess what? Nothing happened. There were no gangs and not a single comment from anyone I walked past. All that fuss over nothing!

The next day was a different matter. I'd simply not been looking in the right direction, so when the trouble started it was completely unexpected. Even more so because it came from my so-called friends.

Jill and I had decided to walk down the path into the grounds and once round the pool before getting changed, just so that we could see who was there. I'd recognised the voice from the stands as soon as we had turned the corner. It was Pete.

"Well, well, there's the yellow bastard now, and 'e's with that Scouse tart again. I told ye I'd seen 'im with 'er last night."

"The turncoat shit!" That was Birdy.

"I'm 'avin' 'im out." Pete said loud enough for me to hear.

"After me."

"And me." And that was Gerry.

They were the three who had separated from us when we were running from the Scousers a couple of weeks earlier. I saw them coming over, but I wasn't going to run. Nothing had happened between us so why should I be worried? Anyway, I wasn't going to look scared in front of Jill.

"Well, what the fuck 'ave we got 'ere then?" Pete said, then pushed me hard in the chest with both hands.

"What's your problem?" I said, taking Jill's arm from mine and pushing her behind me.

"Don't worry, Scouser lover, we're not after ye Scouse bitch."

"Watch your mouth," and Pete received the same push back from me. His face really did register surprise.

"Well, what the fuck do ye know? The yellow bastard is going to fight back. I'm going to enjoy this."

"What do you mean 'yellow bastard'?"

"You know what we fucking well mean. You ran off and left us, and we were caught."

"Well that's your own stupid fault. You had the chance to run away like me, Eddie, and Kev did. So what's the problem?"

"The way we see it, you left us," Birdy said.

"Oh, just me, was it? What about Eddie and Kev?"

"We've already seen to them."

"What, three against one was it?"

"Best way."

"Up yours."

"Oh, you're really going to get it, only much worse."

Pete seemed unbalanced, but there again he had never been one of God's brightest creatures.

"You think so?" I wasn't sure how I was going to stop it, but at least it sounded good. Jill must have been thinking the same thing because she was tugging at my arm, trying to pull me away.

"Oh yeah, ye're 'aving it worse because it'll be like getting a Scouser."

"Really, how do you make that out?"

"The bitch behind ye, ye know, the one tugging at your fucking arm. If ye want to go out with a Scouse slag then ye must be one of them yourself."

That was too much. I smacked Pete in the mouth and I heard his teeth crack. Then my ear seemed to explode as Birdy's fist connected with the side of my head, but I still managed to hit Pete twice more in the face before he went down. All I wanted to do was destroy his mouth for saying those things about Jill. Birdy's second punch caught me on the forehead just before Gerry's kick deadened my right thigh and my leg started to buckle under me.

"Leave him alone, yeh bastards," Jill screamed as she ran forward.

"Fuck off, tart," Birdy shouted and pushed her back against the railings. This gave me chance to grab Gerry by the throat and squeeze.

"Arrh! The bastard's choking me, get the fucker off!"

Birdy, easily the strongest, tried to oblige and punched me in the side of my ribs. I coughed and went down to my knees, but I still squeezed Gerry's throat.

By now Pete had managed to stand again, his mouth dripping blood. "Hold 'im while I kick the shit out of the fucker."

Birdy punched again at my head, splitting my eyebrow, the blood running into my eye and blinding me to the first of Pete's kicks. I tried not to drop any further because if I did the kicks would be aimed at my head. My grip round Gerry's neck gave me support until Birdy lashed out with a swinging kick that drove my arms upwards, breaking my hold. Gerry fell backward gasping, then crawled away as the others continued to kick. There was nothing I could do to stop the kicks anymore and I was sinking lower.

Suddenly I felt a weight over my head and upper body and the kicks stopped. It was Jill! She had thrown herself over me to protect me and was now screaming for help.

"Get the fucking bitch out of the way," Pete shouted, "I want to finish off the Scouse lover."

He never got the chance. Bill Wainright, the Baths' superintendent, had heard the screaming and was less than five yards away when they ran for it.

"You sick buggers," I heard him shout after them. Then he crouched down, "Come on, luv, ye can get up now, they've gone." She was sobbing with fear.

"Let me see 'im."

He helped her up. By then Mavis, one of the kiosk attendants, had arrived, and she put her arm round Jill.

"Bloody 'ell, it's Joe!" I heard Bill say. "Oh God, come on mate. What on earth caused this? Mavis, get that first aid box. Come on, Joe, into the office."

He helped me up, put his arm under my shoulder, and walked me inside.

The incident at the baths had been the final straw. I'd had it with school, I'd had it at home, and my 'mates' had turned as well. Winsford held nothing for me, not even Jill because I'd felt too humiliated about what had happened to ask her out again. Ten days after the fight I had the first of the two interviews. The bruises from the fight had disappeared and I explained my cut eye as a sports injury. I got the job in Altrincham as a trainee surveyor, found a room in a shared flat that had been advertised in the *Manchester Evening News*, and left home. On my last day at school, purely as a final act of defiance, I'd set off the fire alarm, watched as the whole school assembled in the playground, then I walked out of the school gates into a new life.

Chapter 19

I knew that opening the letters would cause you to leave, but your mum couldn't see it. She didn't think it was interfering, only showing an interest. Perhaps it was my fault for not talking to you more and she was overcompensating for me, with you ending up having the worst of both worlds, an interfering mum and a dad who appeared not to give a damn. But how do you start talking to someone after so long of hardly communicating at all? It's like the silence feeds on itself and grows stronger than both of you, so much so that neither of you bother to try any more. I missed you when you left, more than I would ever have imagined possible. And your mum did. Seventeen miles, that's all the distance was to your flat, and yet it might well have been the other end of the country for the number of times you visited us. You never invited us to your flat, we didn't know how you were getting on at work, if you had any friends, girlfriends, what you did, where you went out. It was like a closed part of your life, a complete rebellion against us.

But keep talkin' luv, let me listen just a little bit longer.

New friends had quickly entered my life, from work, from the flat, from college. Oh yes, as part of my training I had to attend day release at the North Cheshire College of Further Education. My four "O" levels had got me onto the Ordinary National Certificate course in Surveying, and I loved it. Can you imagine? Me enjoying day release. Back to school? Not at all. There we were addressed as young adults who wanted to learn. We were treated with respect and not spoken down to as though we were children. And I'd even taken up a sport, ice hockey. My flat was about five minutes away from the Ice Rink in Devonshire Road, and I spent as much of my spare time on the ice as possible. It was hard, fast and tough. I thrived on the excitement and hard training. In a nutshell my new life was brilliant and I never had any desire to waste ice time going back to Winsford for pointless visits.

The shock came at the end of the first year of my O.N.C. I was asked to go to the head of the department's office for a chat. I wondered why because I had no problems and my exam results had been very good.

"Hello Joe," Dr Adams said, offering his hand. We shook. "Take a seat."

He closed the door behind me and took the other visitor's seat rather than his chair behind his desk. His office was lived in, had character you might say. A clear desk policy had obviously never been adopted by Dr Adams. His office reflected him and was clearly an extension of his attitudes: warm, easy-going, comforting. Yes, that was it, comforting. Simon Adams had the ability to make you feel relaxed, and while you never doubted his ability or seriousness, he never pressured people.

"How is the course?"

"I enjoy it."

"Easy, isn't it?"

"There's a lot to do, but the concepts are straightforward enough."

"Even the Maths?"

"Yes, but Maths is straightforward. It's very methodical and clear."

"And boring?"

"Not at all."

"It is for some, in fact, it is for most people. Why not you, Joe?"

"Maybe I have a high boredom threshold."

"I would hardly say that an ice hockey player has a high boredom threshold, would you?" We both laughed at the absurdity of the thought. He then picked up a sheet of paper which had on it a table of some sort.

"Seriously Joe, your Maths results are outstanding. The best I've had in a long time. Easily Distinction category. And the other three subjects, Credits every one. Joe, at this rate you'll sail through your second year and comfortably pass your O.N.C."

"Well, that will be good news for my boss," I said, slightly embarrassed at the praise.

"Oh, it certainly will. But what I am about to suggest won't be." I must have frowned. "Oh no Joe, it's nothing to worry about at all. On the contrary, it would be very good, well, for you at least."

I shifted in the chair, wondering what was coming next.

"You should consider University."

"To read what?" I asked, completely surprised by what he had just suggested.

"Maths!"

"Maths?" Disbelief was clearly evident on my face.

"Why not?" he replied with not a hint of a joke in the tone of his voice. Clearly he was serious, and I replied in the same manner.

"I don't know, I'd just not considered it before. Well, not in Maths, anyway."

"So you *have* thought of University."

"Well no, not really, not since I was about thirteen. And then it was such a long way off. Daydreams, I suppose. Anyway, I realised that I wasn't good enough and I left school. I haven't given it any thought since."

"And how did you know you weren't good enough?"

I shrugged my shoulders slightly. "I suppose it just became obvious to me that I didn't have the ability or intelligence to get there."

"And desire? What happened to the desire to go. You must have had it once because you said you daydreamed of University."

I thought about that for a moment, not really sure how to explain, and not really wanting to explain too much.

"I suppose I just lost the desire somewhere along the way."

He said nothing, and as I looked at him I felt the urge to fill the silence

"I became disillusioned with school, performed badly in my "O" levels, drifted into the sixth form and left."

It was as simple as that. Well, not quite, I left out the home problems.

"What do you think caused your change of attitude to school work?"

Again I shrugged my shoulders, "I don't know. It wasn't just one thing, but I began to feel that I simply wasn't good enough. You know, sometimes you have to acknowledge certain things are true. And it was certainly true that I would not have got to University if I had stayed on at school. I had lost the desire to work, and anyway I had picked stupid subjects for 'A' levels." I grinned and so did he, knowing full well what my choices had been because it was in my file on his desk.

"No, I have to agree that there wasn't any clear link in your choices." He paused for a moment before continuing. "What about your work now, though? Do you simply see it as a means to an end, or is there more?"

"I'm not sure I understand." I was puzzled.

"Is it just for the money that you're now working harder? I know your company awards pay rises if you pass each year, and that you cannot become a qualified surveyor without your Higher National Certificate. But is that the only reason you want to pass?"

"Well, I'd be lying if I said that the pay rise wasn't an incentive to study," to which he smiled and nodded. "But I enjoy my work and want to be a qualified surveyor, so I need to pass anyway."

"Yes," he said, again waving the paper with the results on. "However, these are not just pass marks, these are exceptional marks, too good just for day release and H.N.C. You're doing far more work than is necessary. I know that and you know that. Tell me why, Joe."

"I enjoy it. I enjoy the lectures, I enjoy the projects, I enjoy being taught." The slight nod of his head showed that this was what he had been waiting for.

"Enjoy being taught..." he repeated, as if considering the full implications of what I had said.

"Yes, it's different. The lecturers are different."

"Different from whom?"

"My old teachers."

"But we're still just teachers."

"No, you're not. You have a different approach. You don't speak down to us and you help without being sarcastic."

"Well, thank you for the compliments. Perhaps your approach is different, too. Different from your schooldays. We all change, Joe, and sometimes we can see that a change has occurred because of a single major event. But other times big changes occur because of a series of very small events. The important thing is to recognise that a change *has* occurred. Joe, allow me to digress a little, but keep with me. In our Maths lectures here at the college we very often work through problems using time as a variable, and because of the way we have been systematically taught from childhood, we have a practical concept of time. You know, twenty-four hours in a day, sixty minutes in an hour, that sort of thing." I nodded and listened. "But that is a very naive view leading to such sayings as 'time waits for no man' or 'time is not on my side'. Time will always be on your side if you allow it. Time will allow you the freedom you desire, and will open many doors for you. Equally many doors will also close if time allows."

I could only listen.

"I would say that many things have changed for you over the

past few years since you first dreamed of University, and nine times out of ten a bystander would say that the move away from home was the most significant."

I nodded to this

"Yes, but was it, Joe?"

He stood up and moved slowly round the room, not collecting his thoughts because they were already in place, but allowing himself time — yes time, that was it — he was allowing himself time to decide the best way of speaking to me so that I could understand what he wanted to say.

"To give all the credit for the change in you simply to a move away from home would be wrong."

"Well, it does seem a bit of a coincidence."

"Perfect, absolutely perfect, that was exactly the word I was waiting for." He sat down again, this time leaning forward slightly, his elbows resting on each of the arms of the chair, leaving his hands free to move as he spoke.

"Tell me, Joe, what is a coincidence?"

"I suppose it's when something happens which is odd or that you can't explain."

"So you dismiss it as a coincidence, and leave it at that."

"Most times."

"I would say *every* time with most people."

"I never really thought about it much."

"Who does?"

"You do, don't you?"

"Yes I do. And the more I think about it the more I realise that a coincidence is just another way of saying 'I don't understand the situation'. If we were more aware of everything, there would be fewer coincidences because we would understand what had just happened."

I smiled, not mockingly, but because it sounded a bit far-fetched.

"Okay Joe, here's another one to make you smile. I'm driving my car to the Ice Rink, I've been stuck in bad traffic, I'm late. If I miss this start of the practice I'll be dropped from the squad and I won't play in the next match. I drive round the car park, it's full. I'm feeling anxious, I can feel my heart beating faster. No-one is walking to their cars from the rink. I go round once more, then a car pulls out and I find a space. I get in just in time, secure my place in the squad, and score the first goal of the next match."

This brought a really broad smile to my face.

"It's possible, isn't it?"

"Yes I suppose so."

"And if it happened, what would you say?"

"I would say that was a hell of a coincidence!"

We both laughed.

"Good. Now let's look at it again. Why go round the car park a second time when I hadn't seen anyone walk to their car? It doesn't make sense. It would have made perfect sense to go and try and park on one of the side roads. Tell me, Joe, what made that driver leave? Was it me? Did he sense that I needed the space more than him. What if I was giving out some kind of message and he responded to it."

"But you were giving out a message! You were driving round a car park trying to park!"

"Yes, that's the way it appears on the face of it. Yet if that's all it was, why didn't he move the first time I drove round?"

"He might have thought you were someone who was leaving the car park if he hadn't seen you drive in. There would be no reason to move. But when he saw you coming round a second time he decided to leave so that you could park."

"Why should he leave just on my second drive round, isn't that the coincidence?"

"No, it's like I've just said. He moved when he realised you wanted to park."

"So are you saying that he had probably decided to drive out if I drove round the car park once more, because he was going to leave soon anyway?"

"Yes."

"Well how then did I know to drive round again?"

"You didn't."

"Didn't I? Because we've already agreed that it would have made better sense to look in the side streets to park, so why did I drive round again? Joe, what if I somehow knew that he would move if I went round again?"

"You couldn't know, you hadn't seen him. And even if you had, you wouldn't know what he was thinking."

"Consider this. What if there is a way for things like this to happen that we are not aware of? What if there is a sort of energy, if you like, that allows this to happen? What if we are doing things, without knowing, which bring about a coincidence?"

"I don't know what to say, I'm afraid I'm out of my depth."

"No Joe, no you're not. That's what I'm telling you. It's happening with you, but you simply aren't aware of it. You're probably happy to accept that a big change occurred in you because you left home. Allow me to tell you what I think happened. You found the work interesting so you concentrated a little more instead of idly wasting time. You spent a small amount of time each evening on your college work instead of working only when necessary because it would help you with your work each day. You worked at it little and often, and it became easier to cope with new concepts and ultimately more enjoyable, to the point when you actually looked forward to new problems. With your job and college work firmly in hand, you now felt totally justified in spending as much of your remaining time on the ice as you wanted to. As a result your hockey skills became good enough to make the team. So you see, studying Maths for half an hour each evening has got you into an ice hockey team!"

He smiled, and so did I.

"All too often people are so preoccupied with what they are going to do next, or with what they have just done, that they forget to enjoy what they are doing now. Joe, time is happening now. Use the time now, enjoy things as they happen, don't put things off, and don't dwell on things. Work each day, study each day, play each day, and eventually love each day. Each thing we do adds to a greater picture that we may not be aware of, but day by day it grows. When you first daydreamed about University you were not doing enough related things that would add to the overall picture. But now you are, and without even giving University a single thought during the past twelve months you are now in a position to consider whether you want to go or not. University, Joe, what about it?"

There it was, straight back to it.

"I don't know," I said, fidgeting slightly. "I'm happy in what I'm doing for the first time in ages. I like my job, the course here, and my life outside. I don't think that I want to change anything."

"Yes, I understand that. But give it some thought, Joe. I have no doubt that you'll pass, and pass with very good marks. University is now an open door to you, not a daydream."

"Shouldn't I wait until after H.N.C. and then go? That way I would have finished my training as a surveyor as well."

"A University degree leaves H.N.C. far behind. Don't wait and waste two years, go straight after O.N.C., and then come back and be a surveyor with a degree if you still want to."

"Okay, but maybe I should wait until I get my O.N.C. results next year before I apply. You know, don't count your chickens and all that."

"No. If you don't apply this year you'll never get in next year, and then you'll spend another year kicking yourself for not applying earlier. You need to apply now because University applications are always accepted and processed one year in advance."

"I don't know," I said weakly.

"If I didn't think you were capable of this you wouldn't be sitting here now. Believe me, I would love you to take H.N.C. in my department because I know that you'd pass, and you're a pleasure to teach. But I also know that I would not be acting in your interests if I didn't advise you to apply to University."

He sat and watched me. I said nothing, this time leaving him to fill the silence.

"I advise you with all my heart to apply now to study for a Bachelor of Science degree in Maths. I'll help you to make choices regarding courses and Universities if you like, but apply now, obtain a place. And then if next year you don't want to go, don't go. Give the place up, because someone else will gladly fill it. At least by applying now you give yourself the option of what to do next year. Who knows, the desire to go might have been awakened."

He stood up, the time he was prepared to give me was over. Now it was up to me. I nodded and stood.

"Give it some thought, Joe, you'll really enjoy life as a student. It's very much like the life you're leading now and you could always choose a University with an ice rink nearby. No point in giving up the hockey, is there?"

"None at all," I agreed. I turned to leave.

"One last thing, Joe. Doors will open and close all through your life, and time will sometimes appear to be on your side and sometimes against you. The door to University is open to you today and can be kept open for another year. It is up to you to close it today, next year, or walk through it. Will it ever open again if you close it, who can say. I don't believe in predestination, but I do know that things happen as a result of coincidences. And I believe that they should not be ignored. Tell me, Joe, did the man move from the car park so that I could score the goal or park my car? Isn't one just the extension of the other, inextricably linked by coincidence?"

Chapter 20

*Y*our lecturer at Altrincham was a wise man, and although his ideas might have seemed strange to you then, I don't think now they are strange at all.

It all seems so clear now, how every little event was contributing to a greater event, and even that greater event was only part of something else. And he was right about predestination. Everything isn't set out for us, we don't live our lives where everything was meant to happen. We can change things, and everything we do will cause a small change. After each meeting, each action, nothing will be the same again, and we always have a choice. Sometimes one, sometimes many, and each choice, each action, may produce a different result, or maybe the same result in a different way. Some may take longer, some more direct, it's all a matter of time. Everything is a matter of time, but like your lecturer said, do we really know what time is?

I know I never gave it much thought, but if I had to guess I would say it was a kind of energy, an energy that gets things done. I can't remember how many times I must have said "I haven't got the time" when really what I meant was I didn't have the energy or the inclination. It fits when you say it like that, doesn't it? And yet other times, now there's a funny use of the word, we get lots of things done because we have the time for them. But what we really mean is that we have the energy for them, the hours and minutes are probably just the same as before.

How did we lose time for each other, Joe? How can the energy between a father and son fade after being so strong? Let me answer, because tonight I know. It fades little by little, and each little action adds to a greater action, and so it builds until it seems like it's insurmountable. Yet it isn't. It can be changed at any moment by one little action, one little piece of energy, one small fraction of time. Then the picture will begin to change and ultimately become a different picture than was previously being painted. It seems so clear now that I wonder if it's really me thinking these things. Am I really only waking up on the night I'm going to die?

We almost changed it the summer that you graduated, and for a few months I really thought we were drawing closer together. We had both made the effort over your graduation day. You had invited me even though you had expected me to say no, and I had said that I would come despite being petrified at the thought of it. Of course, your mum had booked her seat three years earlier on your first day of Freshers Week, and nothing would have stopped her watching you graduate and attending the wine and cheese party with the lecturers afterward. For me it was nerve-racking. The thought of walking into a University was intimidating enough, but to talk with your lecturers, I mean, what could I possibly say to them that would be interesting.

I remember walking across the Old Quadrangle and through the arched oak doors into the main hall. The building was beautiful, old, carved and with spires, just like I'd imagined a University would look like. I loved it and yet my stomach was turning over I was so nervous. I felt completely out of my depth.

Your mum knew what I was feeling and she squeezed my hand as we took our seats and waited for the Graduands to walk in. We strained our necks to see you, just like parents at their child's first nativity play. I wondered how nervous you must be, and then I saw your smiling face. You were so at ease as you walked in with all your fellow students, mortar boards under your arms, and not a care in the world. You were totally relaxed in these surroundings. It was your world and I was visiting for a day. After I saw you sit down my nervousness left me. It was as though your confidence became mine and you were looking after me.

When all the Graduands had been called out and presented with their degrees, the parade took place. I remember you all standing, now wearing the mortar boards of Graduates, and walking down the centre aisle. I couldn't have been more proud, and when you walked past, smiled at your mum, and winked at me as if to say "look at me now, Dad!" I knew we had something to build on and things weren't too late for us.

In the years after you had left home your mum really did change, and she never made the same mistakes with Rose. When Rose didn't want to speak or she needed her privacy, it was respected, and our house was more peaceful. Rose owed you a great deal for that, Joe. I knew that deep down your mum hoped that someday you would move back home, but I knew it wouldn't happen. I knew from the day you left any further contact would be with an independent young man. I just wish it hadn't been so infrequently.

Perhaps if you had taken a bit more time off after graduating we might have had more of a chance. One week didn't seem very much after so many exams. But all the same, I'm glad you stayed with us for that week before you took your new job offshore. It meant a lot to your mum and to me. If only it had been longer.

It would have been good to have had a longer break after I'd graduated but I'd accepted a position in the oil industry as an offshore surveyor, and the offer had depended on me starting immediately. I hadn't wanted to lose the opportunity because it seemed like the job offered the best of all worlds: based in Singapore, tax free salary, and six months off every year.

Before the end of that one week break I'd looked up one or two old friends. Nige was still around and had hardly changed, but on the whole Winsford had no hold on me. On the Thursday before I left, my graduation photographs were delivered and I'd taken one round to Uncle Thomas as I'd always promised I would. Well, actually I'd promised Aunty Joan, but she had died one month before I graduated so she never saw it.

Uncle Thomas had taken it and immediately placed it in the space that had been reserved for it three years earlier, pride of place in the centre of the mantelpiece. He'd stood back to admire, but in his face I'd seen how Aunty Joan's death had affected him. There had been far too much weight loss.

"She was so proud, you know, she kept telling them all at the chapel that you were the first in the family to go to University and would be the first to get a degree. She never doubted you would graduate, none of us did. You know, as a boy people tried to make your mind up for you and you wouldn't have it. But once you'd made it up yourself there was no stopping you."

He gave a little smile and then turned to gaze out of the window, looking at, but not seeing, his neglected rose garden. His eyes were empty, just like his life. He was taking her death very badly. I felt helpless, what could I say to someone who had lost their partner after all those years together? Should I stay with him or go? What would help him?

"Have you got any Murray Mints, left Uncle Thomas?"

He turned and grinned at me, then went to the cupboard in the corner.

"One or two?" he asked.

"Let's try for three, shall we. I'm a grown-up now," I said smiling, the joke not lost on him. Then he started to cry. I stood up and put my arm on his shoulder while he steadied himself

"I'll be all right. Come on, sit down. Let's see if you can manage all three."

So we sat in the quiet sucking Murray Mints. I never saw Uncle Thomas again. He died two months later and left me his house.

I managed to get back to Winsford about four weeks after he died, and I'd stayed in my house for the first time. I'd only been able to take ten days leave but I'd thought that would've been long enough anyway. I'd decided it would have been a good idea for my mum and dad to move into the house.

"Well, it's there to be lived in. It doesn't make sense for it to stand empty. I'm based in the Far East now Dad, I don't need it," I'd said.

"Sell it, then."

"What for? I don't need the money. Why don't you want to move in."

"Because we don't want to. Anyway the garden is a bit small. Ye know what I'm like about gardening," he said, trying to make a bit of a joke of it.

"It's not just you though, is it? What about mum and Rose. I'm sure they'd like to move."

"Rose 'as gone off to University so it doesn't concern 'er, and me and your mum are all right where we are for the time being."

"But you wouldn't have any rent to pay."

"What about ye if ye move back? It would be there for ye."

"Dad, I won't be coming back to Winsford. I work away now."

"Maybe not forever."

"Look Dad, I've got a good job. I like it. And even if I did get fed up with travelling, I wouldn't move back to Winsford."

"Why, isn't it good enough for ye now? Do ye look down on us now that ye've got a degree and ye're in the oil industry."

"Dad, are you forgetting I'd moved away long before I ever went to University."

"No, I'm not forgetting. I just 'oped that was in the past now."

He looked sad when he said it, like an old wound had started to open up.

"It is, it is. I don't mean that I hate Winsford, it's just that moving back would seem like a real step backwards."

"Yeah, maybe you're right. Different times, eh?"

He looked round his garden, already tidy ready for the onset of winter, and I looked at him.

"I remember being away, and all I could think about every night was getting back to Winsford. Strange isn't it? I know there's never been much 'ere, but I've always loved this town. For all it's faults. Maybe wars cloud your vision, and ye don't see things as they really are."

"Maybe that's the point, Dad, maybe you do see things for what they are. And if that's what you want, then that's good enough. It just isn't what I want."

We looked in each other's eyes and both understood, both feeling sad at how things had been, but both realising that those times were gone, and things that had happened could not be undone.

"Your mum will be disappointed if she 'ears you say that ye're never coming back."

"Then let's not tell her. Let her believe that there's always the possibility. Why upset her?"

"Yeah, why?"

"How about the house, then?" I tried once more.

"No, I don't think so."

"Then you will think about it?"

"No, There's no point —"

"No, point —"

"Let me finish, Joe. We've got other plans, and we're almost ready to sign."

I looked confused.

"We're buying old Mrs Daniel's house."

Now I was surprised. He hadn't said a word about it before now. "We were going to tell ye about it before ye went back, but I'd better tell ye now, otherwise ye won't understand why we don't want to live in your 'ouse. It's not that I'm not grateful of the offer, I am, and yer mum will be when I tell 'er what ye've said, but we've been planning this for a while. We would've let ye know in a letter, but there's been so many problems to sort out, that a couple of times we thought it would all fall through."

"You'll like it there, it's got a big garden," was all I could say. I had to admit that I felt a little hurt that he hadn't told me before.

What would it have changed if I'd have known? But really, what else could I have expected. Not telling each other things was nothing new. A legacy of our younger days, you might say.

"Yeah, it 'as, but yer mum's really fond of the 'ouse. She remembers when we lived there with granddad Joseph when we were first married. There's a lot of nice memories for us as a young couple setting out in our life together, and a lot of 'appy memories for yer mum about 'er dad."

"That's good."

"Yeah, so what will ye do about your 'ouse then?"

"I don't know now. I thought you would've said 'yes' to moving in."

"Well leave it a while before ye make a decision. Ye mum'll keep it tidy, and I'll see to the garden. There's no rush to do anything, is there?"

Chapter 21

I stirred in the chair, my back creaking as much as the chair did. What a restless night, and dreams. I'd never had such vivid dreams. Each time I'd closed my eyes I'd seemed to be reaching back to a different part of my life. I'd wanted to sit with my dad and watch over him, and yet my night had been spent going over past arguments. I didn't want to remember him that way.

Through the window the night sky was beginning to fade, the darkness becoming lighter in anticipation of the dawn. The birds in the large bush had become restless. The night was almost over, and yet it had seemed only moments ago that they had gone to roost. I remember looking at the sky as it had changed, from deep black with beautiful stars through different shades of blue, becoming ever lighter as the sun removed the colours, almost like a painting left in continual sunlight until all the colours faded. Except I knew the night sky would be replaced by a beautiful dawn. And I realised I'd seen this before. Once I had sat out all night under the Red Sea sky waiting for the dawn and the ominous journey home, knowing that at the end of the journey would be heartache.

The survey work had finished for the day and we had tied up at Ras Gemsa for the night. We were working amongst the coral reefs at the top of the Red Sea where the Gulf of Suez began. It was still a politically sensitive area and so night-time movement was not allowed. Still, for us that was a bonus. Normally we would be working a twenty-four hour operation, so it was a nice change to be only working daylight hours, especially on this vessel. As the saying goes, "every cloud has a silver lining" and our use of this vessel had come about entirely because a company specialising in diving holidays had gone bust and the vessel had been impounded in the Red Sea port of Hurghada. We had been looking for a survey vessel to conduct the work between the reefs, and she was ideal. For us the boat had been a gift from the gods. *Jacia* was the sister ship of the *Calypso*, Jacques Cousteau's boat, and she was kitted out for holidaymakers. A gin palace. Excellent.

We had been there for two weeks when the call came through. I had been called from the lounge bar to the bridge to take a call which would change my world in a way I would never have dreamed. I'd taken the radio handset, and through the static of the SSB I'd heard the voice of the shore controller, Bill Turney.

"Joe, can you hear me, Joe?" The line was very poor.

"Two by two, go ahead."

"Joe...." Crackling static. "I have... terrible news..." then the line became crystal clear. "Your mother has died." Then more static.

I said nothing. I stared, not believing, unable to take it in. She was too young, it was a mistake. She wasn't ill.

"Joe, are you still there, Joe?"

Mick, one of the engineers, took the handset from me.

"He got the message, Bill. We'll deal with it now. *Jacia* out." He clipped the handset back on the receiver.

"Come and sit down, mate, I'll get you a drink."

"No, no drink, I need a clear head. I have to get off. I need to go back home. My dad won't be able to cope. I have to leave. Look, I'm going to sit outside. I'll be all right, but I need to be alone."

"Sure, mate, of course. We'll call the rig and try to get you on the first chopper to Hurghada airport in the morning. Give me a shout if you need anything, anything at all."

That night I'd watched the sky change. I'd looked round for stars I might recognise and saw the Plough constellation. It had made me feel better in a childlike way because I'd often been able to see it from our garden in the cottages. It made me feel closer to home. The strangest feeling of all that night was that as I watched the stars I didn't feel alone.

At six o'clock the next morning my bags were carried to the aft deck by one of the ship's crew, a local Egyptian.

"You need to be very strong for your father, he needs you more than ever now," he said to me, then shook my hand. Two weeks ago the man had been a complete stranger, now I would never forget him.

I was transferred by basket to the drillship and caught the first chopper ashore. They were using a bubble helicopter for shuttle work and the flight to shore over the coral reefs was magnificent. Such beauty. At Hurghada airport I was met by Bill, the shore controller, who had somehow obtained my passport from the port immigration office during the night. How, I don't know. I never asked and I never cared.

At Cairo airport I was rushed through the security checks, all five of them, without my baggage so that I could catch the British Airways flight to Heathrow. I was one of the last to board the plane and a stewardess asked if I was Mr Harrison. I nodded.

"If there is any assistance we can give you, please let us know. You will be met at Heathrow and taken to Terminal One for the shuttle flight to Manchester. You should just make it if we can rush you through customs." She smiled again. I thanked her and went to find my seat.

Five and a quarter hours later we landed at Heathrow and the plane taxied to a halt. The flight hadn't been too bad, but now it seemed that the nearer I got to home the worse I felt. All along I hoped it was mistake, but the closer I was the more I knew it was real. We stood and queued in the aisle. There was an announcement: "Would Mr Harrison please make himself known to the attendant who is waiting to escort him through customs. Thank you."

The two men in front shuffled impatiently, and the one directly in front of me made the mistake of saying to the other "How many more fucking announcements are there going to be for this Mr Harrison? That's all we heard in the waiting area in Cairo. Who the fuck is he? That's what I'd like to know."

I felt sorry for him. Sorry for his lack of understanding, sorry that he could judge so quickly without knowing the reasons. I tapped him on the shoulder and he turned.

"I'm Mr Harrison, and if you knew the reason for the announcements I'm sure you wouldn't be so quick to complain. However, because I can't be bothered to tell an arsehole like you, I'll just advise you to shut the fuck up before I break your jaw."

He flushed, his friend looked away. Caught out, he tried to apologise. "Look, I, er, I didn't mean... it's just that...." When he looked in my eyes he stopped making excuses. "I'm sorry."

I looked away from him, no longer interested.

I made the flight to Manchester with minutes to spare. The face of the man who had complained kept flashing through my mind. He had been too quick to condemn, he hadn't cared what the reasons might have been, he simply needed to condemn. And then I realised who it reminded me of. It was me, it was how I had been with my dad, always too quick to judge, never giving an inch.

Seeing it in someone else had driven it home to me. But what was I to do now? How would I speak to my dad? I simply didn't know. Had too much water gone under the bridge? It had been over two years since my mum and dad had moved house, and in all that time I had only visited once, during a weekend break in a computing course I'd had to attend in Manchester. What would I say to him?

The taxi had dropped me outside the front door, but I'd walked round to the back door, knowing that it would be open. I walked in without knocking. He was sitting in his chair by the fireplace and he slowly looked up, expecting just another visitor. Then he'd realised it was me. I'd never seen such sadness in a face, and never wanted to again.

He'd stood up and walked over to me, slowly at first, had raised his arms, and the look on his face changed to longing. He needed comfort, and for the first time since I'd been eleven years old I'd hugged my dad and we'd cried in each other's arms.

The memory of it had made my eyes glassy again, causing the light of dawn to sparkle from the window. I'd always wished that things had been different and that somehow, if I had still been at home, I could have saved my mum from the single heart attack that had killed her. Perhaps if I'd been able to resuscitate her, maybe start her heart again, just until the ambulance could have got there.... Perhaps if I had found her sooner then she wouldn't have died. What if the basic first aid I had learned on survival courses would have been the key? I doubted if my dad would have known what to do. If only I had been there. Those were the torments that continually came back to haunt me. If only I had been there.

It wouldn't have done any good, Joe. There's no point in going over it. I tried, believe me, I tried. I knew what to do, and I've no doubt I knew far more first aid than you did so don't blame yourself. Listen Joe, for over six years I had been the shift first aider and been on countless courses, and for the last two years before your mum died I had been the safety officer for all three shifts. It had taken me a long time to realise that I could manage more difficult

172

jobs, but through first aid, which I seemed to have a knack for, I was promoted. That was the reason I stopped working shiftwork, and that was why we could afford to buy our own house. You'd moved away by then, and on the few occasions when we'd met, the subject never came up in conversation. We hardly spoke in those days, did we?

Anyway, that night we had been watching the television. Most of the evening. Your mum hadn't been her normal lively self all day and hadn't said much all night, which was unusual, and at ten o'clock she said she was going to have an early night. She kissed me goodnight and went up the stairs. Ten minutes later I heard a bang — no, it was more, it was a heavy thump on the bedroom floor. I raced up the stairs and when I ran into the bedroom your mum was crumpled on the floor, not moving. Her lips were blue and I knew immediately it was a heart attack. I felt for a pulse in her neck. Nothing!

"No, Vi!" I shouted. Then my training kicked in. I laid her flat out and started to pump her chest, 1 - 2 - 3 - 4 - 5, then two breaths of air, 1 -2 - 3 - 4 - 5, two breaths.

"Breathe Vi, please!" I couldn't go back downstairs to the phone, I couldn't leave her. I pumped her chest, gave more air, and checked her pulse again. Nothing. Please breathe, please breathe! Christ, it wasn't working! I needed to get an ambulance. What could I do? I quickly dragged her to the door, to the top of the stairs, then swept her up into my arms and rushed down the stairs, stumbling on the last step, going down on my knees in the hall, holding her tight. I dragged her along the floor to the phone table, grabbed the receiver and dialled 999.

"Ambulance," I said and gave the address.

I carried on trying to revive her, five minutes, ten minutes, fifteen minutes, until the night filled with the sound of sirens and blue lights flashed through the glass in the front door to the hall. I opened the door before they knocked, and went back to her.

"We'll take over now," a voice said. I looked up.

"Heart attack," I managed to say. "Save her, please. I've tried, God knows I've tried."

"Let us to her."

I slumped on the stairs, out of breath, light-headed, my arms by my side, palms up. I saw one shake his head to the other and I knew. He turned to me.

"I'm sorry—"
"No! No! No, no, no—"
Then I lay back and my chest felt tight, tight, TIGHT!

Whoosh!
My head jerked round to the window. The sound was incredible. The agitation of all the birds in the bush had finally reached a crescendo and then, as if by some magical signal, they had all taken flight together. It had startled me and I'd looked to my dad to see that it hadn't disturbed him.

"Nurse! Nurse!" I shouted, jumping out of my chair and reaching for the buzzer. He was lying back with his arms outstretched, the nebuliser mask off and his mouth wide open. His chest was heaving but he couldn't breathe. His mouth kept gaping, trying to take in air, like a fish out of water. I shouted again. I pressed the buzzer. Christ, where was she? Then she ran in.

"Oh my God! Marion!" she shouted outside. "Quickly! Stand back, Mr Harrison."

I watched from the corner of the room as they gave him another injection. Except that this time it was larger.

"I hope we're in time."

I watched the liquid being squeezed into his veins, knowing that whilst the immediate effect would help him to live, the ultimate effect of the drug was to decrease his resistance and help him to die. Giving with one hand, yet taking away with the other. His breath came back in short gasps, each gradually getting longer, until the pain disappeared from his face and he was breathing easier. Easier for a man dying of lung failure, that is.

The nurse turned to me.

"Have you thought about what I said before, Mr Harrison, because he really needs small doses at regular intervals from now on if we're to prevent him from having a particularly stressful time."

Say 'yes', Joe, say 'yes'. Now is the time, believe me. I don't want that feeling again.

"Mr Harrison, you really do have to think about your dad."

'Yes', Joe, 'yes'.

I looked at his face, so much more peaceful than it had been a few minutes ago. I felt pressure on my hand. Did he squeeze it? No, he looked asleep now. He wasn't moving.

I did squeeze, Joe, but I can't move. I can't speak or open my eyes. Only my mind can move now.

"Yes, do it," I said.

"Nurse, fetch the needle, tube, and control pump, would you please. Believe me," she said looking directly at me, "you've made the right decision, and eventually you'll be glad you did."

She took my arm and guided me to the door, turning away from the bed as she spoke, as if not wanting my dad to hear, although I very much doubted that he was aware of anything that was going on any more.

Oh, I am Joe, I'm more aware tonight than I have ever been in my life. Something's happening to me, and it isn't just dying, or maybe that's exactly what it is! Maybe it happens to everyone when they die. Tonight I have been laying my demons to rest.

"Mr Harrison, your dad doesn't have much longer to live. Perhaps a few hours at the most. If you want any other members of the family to see him then you should really phone them now. Why not do it now while we fit the tube. You can use the phone on my desk."

I nodded and left the room. I made two calls, the first to my wife, and the second to Rose.

"It's me."

"Are you all right?" Emma asked.

175

"Not really."

"Has Sam—?"

"No, but it may not be long off."

"I'll take the children to my mum's and I'll come straight away."

"Okay, just drive carefully."

"I will. I love you."

"I love you, too."

Click.

Then I was on the phone to my sister.

"Rose, it's Joe."

"How is he?"

"You'd better come now, and bring Michael with you, you'll need him."

"We'll be straight there."

Click.

I stared at the phone. Odd really, I thought, after all these years Rose and I still lived locally. You would have thought that with both of us going away to University at least one of us would have settled somewhere else. But no, we were both back in Cheshire, different towns, yet still here.

I went back down the corridor to my dad's room. The door was open and the nurse was waiting by the bed. She held a rectangular box in her hand. When she spoke her voice was not cold, but very matter of fact.

"What will happen, Mr Harrison, is that your dad will now find it increasingly more difficult to relax as his remaining lung capacity diminishes. This will cause his chest to tighten, which will put more pressure on his lung, and reduce even further the available air space left. It is a most vicious circle. Whenever you see him starting to fight and gasp you must press the red button, here. This will cause the syringe to depress and administer a regulated dose. Initially one press should be enough, but as the lung fills with fluid, he'll fight more, and you'll have to press the button two or three times in order to help him to relax. The fact that your dad is a strong-willed individual, and obviously a fighter to the end, means that he will only make things harder for himself and for you as he loses his battle to live. Be brave and hold his hand. I assure you he'll know that you're helping him."

"But what about the nebuliser?" I asked. "Shouldn't he have that as well?"

"I'm afraid he is beyond that now. Remember, I'll be right outside."

She turned and left.

I stood by the bed, still holding his hand while he slept, aware of
the needle now protruding from his vein connecting to the tube
connecting to the box that administered the drug that would help
him to die. And I was the one who was to press the button. I felt
lost. I needed Emma, I needed my wife by me.

*She's coming now Joe, I can hear her footsteps in the corridor.
Don't worry, she'll help you. And Rose is at the main entrance now.
Michael has just put his arm round her as they walked through the
doors.*

Emma's eyes filled with tears as she walked in and saw me holding my dad's hand.

*Hello, luv, you sit with him. He's had a long night. No, don't cry,
I look worse than I feel and the drugs are helping me to relax. I'm
not frightened any more. Joe's with me and he's helping me. We've
been talking all night, haven't we, Joe?*

"I'm glad you're here. He hasn't got much time left. He's not
opened his eyes all night."

"Oh Joe, I'm sorry," she said as she kissed my cheek and touched
my hair.

*He's a good lad, Emma, you look after him. I can tell he worships
you, has ever since he met you. It was funny, you know, to see him
behaving like that. You could see that he had fallen for you straight
away. Who would have thought it. Such a coincidence, but there
again what is a coincidence?*

Chapter 22

"How much time can ye 'ave off work, Joe?" my dad asked. "It's been two weeks since the funeral, don't ye 'ave to be getting back?"

"I've got quite a lot of leave due, so I'm okay for another four weeks. Anyway, don't you be thinking about that. You need some company, so I'm staying for a while. And you can't go back to work yet either. Not until the doctor signs you off."

"'E doesn't know what 'e's talkin about. I'm not suffering from acute depression, I'm upset because your mum 'as died, that's all."

"That's all? Well, I've heard everything now."

"Well, I mean, they want to make it into something it's not. Can't I just be sad for a while and then slowly come to terms with it? Bloody doctors."

"Are you missing work? Would you be better off going back?"

"No, not in the slightest. I've 'ad enough of working down there. Me and your mum 'ad talked about me taking early retirement. I've got a good pension built up, and if I took 'alf of it in cash I could pay off what I owe on the 'ouse and still live comfortably."

"Are you still going to?"

"I don't know yet. Maybe I would be better off working. But to be 'onest, there's no reason for me to carry on with it now. I might as well spend my time doing what I want for whatever time I've got left. Who would 'ave thought it, eh? She wasn't even sixty."

"I know Dad." I put my hand on his shoulder. It helped a little.

"Anyway, what about yer 'ouse. It is 'abitable yet?"

"Sort of."

"And the garden?"

I smiled. "The garden's all right because you've been growing vegetables in it."

"Well, it seemed a shame to just grow roses in that good soil, especially when no-one was going to see them," he replied with a slight grin. "Are ye out tonight?"

"Yeah, I'm meeting one of my old mates from school, Nige. Do you remember him?"

"I remember 'im, cheeky bugger 'e was. Said I was getting fat when I saw 'im once."

"He said that?"

"Well, 'e said I was putting on a bit of lard round the waist."

I laughed. "And were you?"

"Only a bit, but I soon lost it after that."

"I'll remind him about that when I see him."

"Where are ye going, anywhere I know?"

"Yeah, they've done up the Oak at the bottom of Winsford, called it the Bees Knees. From the outside it looks lively, the beer garden is always full. Maybe I'll see some others I know."

"All right then. See ye tomorrow?"

"Yeah, I'll call in the morning."

"Okay. See ye, Joe."

I left and walked up to my house. He didn't seem too bad. He was coping far better than I ever expected him to, and we were managing to talk to each other without arguing which was a major improvement. Nothing special, but at least talking.

The pub was really busy when I arrived. Even from the bridge I could see that most of the tables in the beer garden were already full, and it looked just as packed inside.

"Oi, Woollyback Joe! Over 'ere."

Lots of heads turned to see who had shouted, and then they turned in my direction to see who he was shouting at. Typical, bloody typical. My face must have been scarlet as I walked across the road and through the gate to Nige's table.

"Thanks, mate."

"Don't mention it, just get 'em in."

He banged his empty pint pot on the table. "Your round already."

"Cheers, Nige."

"Mine's Blackthorn cider, and Ian is drinking Guinness. Yeh have what yeh like."

"Hello, Ian, I'm Joe."

"Yeh, I just 'eard."

Big grin.

"He's a star, isn't he?" I nodded in Nige's direction, raising my eyebrows at the same time. Then I made my way through the crowds to the bar.

Fifteen minutes later I was served. Three pints in hand I turned from the bar and saw her. Slim, light brown hair, tight jeans, *very* fitted white vest top with lace trim, and a face that stopped me dead. I stared.

"Are you moving, mate? I'm dying of thirst 'ere," the man next to me said as he elbowed his way to the bar.

"Oh, er, yeah, sure. Sorry." I moved, she stood still, waiting by one of the high round tables. Waiting for her boyfriend, I'd bet. Fat chance that she would be on her own. She saw me looking but turned away.

"Hey, who do yeh think you're starin' at!"

There was a hint of a threat in the voice, but it was a woman's, and I thought I recognised it.

"Come on, Joe, look at me. I said who do yeh think you're starin' at?"

I turned and I couldn't believe it. "Jill!"

"Long time no see. In fact, very long time no see."

She stood and gave me the once over.

"Well, you've certainly filled out. Look at these muscles," she said, putting her hands on either side of my shoulders.

"And so have you," I replied, giving her a quick head to toe look.

"Cheeky! I've always been this good, as well yeh know, and stop avoidin' my question."

"What question?"

"I said who are yeh starin' at?"

"No-one now that I've seen you again," I joked.

"Well that's good. Because if I thought that yeh were givin' my little sister the eye, I'd 'ave to warn 'er off."

My face dropped. "You're joking, of course?"

"Not on your life. That's Emma, and I'm lookin' after 'er tonight."

"She's stunning."

"I know, that's why she needs a big sister to look out for 'er. Me!"

"And why aren't you out with someone tonight?"

She held up her left hand. "Because my 'usband plays darts on Friday nights, and I go out with the girls. Except they've gone clubbin' tonight and I didn't fancy it."

"You could introduce me."

"Get lost, yeh wouldn't stand a chance."

She laughed and walked over to her sister, and I walked out into the garden, beers in hand. I glanced at Emma again and this time she was looking. I was certain there was a little smile.

"Well, about time and all. Where've ye been?"

"Nige, you sound more like a Woollyback than I do now."

"I told ye we'd take over."

"It sounds like you've been taken over, more like."

"Ian, when ye went to the toilet, who was Woollyback Joe talkin' to?"

"Jill."

"Really! Well, we'll 'ave to 'ave words with 'er later about 'olding up our beer deliveries. It's too 'ot at night for that talking nonsense. Next time you go, Ian, it'll be quicker."

"Bollocks to that. It's your round next, yeh sneaky sod!"

"My oh my, I do declare. Can't you just tell that he never went to the Grammar School. What say you, Joseph?" Nige asked as he pretended to pick his nose with his little finger.

We squirmed. "You disgusting animal. Stop it."

"Jesus, how will we ever attract any of the opposite sex to our table?"

"Ask Joe. 'E's a regular man of the world, aren't yeh, Joe? Yeh'll guide us, won't yeh. Go on, show us country folk 'ow to do it."

"Sod off, Nige."

But he wasn't going to give up. Once one of his funny moods took over you might as well wait for him to rest. That was how he had been at school, but now he was even worse because he could do accents.

"Tell yeh what, why don't I go and ask Jill and 'er sister to come and join us. Yeh'd like that wouldn't yeh."

"Don't do this to me, Nige, for fuck's sake."

And that was the mistake. I'd said it too seriously. They both picked up on it, and like a pair of glove puppets Nige and Ian immediately stopped everything, turned and stared at each other, put their hands on their cheeks, and shook their heads.

"He's in love," Nige said.

"The boy's in love."

"Oh deary, deary me."

"The boy's in love," said Ian.

Then they turned to me, eyes almost popping out, mouths wide open with their hands at the sides of their faces. In harmony they said, "We're going to get 'er, we're going to get 'er." And they left the table.

In less than a minute Nige and Ian appeared with Jill and Emma in tow. I was laughing as the young women tried to resist, but it was no use.

"Jill, yeh know Joe, don't yeh?" Nige asked.

She nodded.

"But you don't, do yeh?" he said to the now embarrassed Emma, who shook her head.

"Please, ignore my *friends*," I offered.

"We're not your *friends*," Ian copied, "tonight we are— chaperones, aren't we Nige?"

"Ooooh, what a lovely word. Yes, that's what we are."

Their heads went together, and they looked skywards, fluttering their eyelashes.

"Oh, very good, very good."

"Come on, Emma," Jill said, "we might as well sit down. It looks like it's going to be a lively table with these two. And Joe, if 'e decides to say 'ello." She looked at me and smiled.

"Joe meet Emma, Emma meet Joe. Right, there yeh are, yeh've been introduced, so yeh can talk to each other, but no touchy touchy."

"Shut up, Nige."

But it was funny, and it was hard not to laugh with him when he was like this.

The next day, Saturday, we had our first date, and on Sunday I borrowed my dad's car and we went out to North Wales for the day, ending up eating chicken with chilled white wine next to the rocks in Erias Park at Colwyn Bay. That night before I took her home we called to see my dad.

"Dad there's someone I want you to meet. Dad, this is Emma." I remember him standing up, his face beaming, I would never have believed it would mean so much to him.

"I'm very pleased to meet ye, luv," and he shook her hand. He was so nice to her, talking without prying, just being my dad and helping me and Emma to feel comfortable.

Over the next few weeks I saw her as often as possible. In fact I spent most of the days just looking forward to the evenings when I would meet her. By the end of the second week I knew I had to start looking around. This time with Emma would end soon unless I did something about it. But what? I now worked in the survey industry based in the Far East. There were not many openings for me in rural Cheshire. By the end of the third week I had a plan.

The odd thing was, it wasn't me who brought the subject up, it was my dad. We were standing by his greenhouse, having a well-earned cup of tea after I'd moved some flagstones for him and he had been the foreman to see that they were put in the right place.

"One more week, Joe."

I looked at him, knowing exactly what he meant.

"What will ye do?"

"I don't know, I can't imagine not seeing her again."

"Yeah, she's quite a catch, isn't she."

"You can say that again."

"Maybe ye could still see each other between trips. Ye've still got yer own 'ouse to come back to."

I shook my head. "Some of the surveys are up to two months long, and I have to be based in Singapore because that's where the office is. It's a condition of the contract."

"Oh," he nodded and looked around the garden waiting, for me to continue.

"I wouldn't want that anyway. I want to see her more than that. It would drive me mad not seeing her for that length of time."

"Yeah, it's 'ard not seeing someone ye love."

His eyes dropped just for a moment, and he let the feeling stay with him until it was time for it to go.

"I'm not going back."

I waited for his reaction to me giving up such a good job. It didn't come.

"It doesn't surprise me. I wouldn't leave a girl like 'er. They don't come knocking on yer door very often. Once in a lifetime is as much as ye can hope for. She's 'ere now Joe, and it's your choice."

"What do you think she thinks of me?"

"What?" His eyebrows lifted. "Do ye really need me to tell ye?"

"No. No I don't."

"So what will ye do? What work can ye get round 'ere?"

"I'm not sure I can get work."

"Ye could always be a teacher."

"No thanks, Dad. I have a very different view of teachers than I think you have."

"What then?"

"I've been thinking about doing something on my own."

"Such as?"

"I've been doing some looking round, at properties, you know.

Small terraced ones, checking prices and things, and I've been thinking about buying a couple of 'two up two downs' with no bathrooms and doing them up, selling them at a profit, and then buying more to do the same thing."

"Sounds risky."

"No, it's not. Look, I know from my time years ago about commercial property, and this is only lower league stuff. I wouldn't need to borrow money, either."

"No?"

"No. Why should I? I already have a house that was left to me, and for the last two years I've worked abroad on a good salary that was tax free. I have enough cash to buy two old houses and renovate them, and live okay for the next six months."

"Well, it seems like ye 'ave it planned out already."

"Yes, I have. In fact, I sign for the first house on Friday!"

He grinned, "That's just like you. But you know, it's funny. Me and your mum always thought that ye would meet someone at University, get married, and never come back. 'Ow odd that ye should meet someone 'ere in Winsford, and a girl who came from Liverpool!"

"It's a good job the Scousers came, Dad."

We both gave a laugh at the irony of that.

"But Dad, don't tell her why I'm doing all this. If she asks, say I was planning to do it all along. I don't want any pressure on her. Then if things don't work out between us, if she gets fed up, it will be easier for her to call it a day."

"She won't."

"Just promise, Dad."

"All right, I promise not to, but on the condition that ye promise to tell 'er on the day ye get married."

"Okay, it's a deal."

I told her two years later on the day we were married.

Chapter 23

*P*ush the button, Joe. Joe! Quick! Good. That's it. Good. Take it easy, breathe slowly. Slowly. My breathing is getting harder and harder, like there's no place for the air to go. Have to keep calm. Oh no, it's coming again. Press again Joe, quick! Yes, that's it. Good, that's much better.

Yeah Joe, you really fell on your feet with the old houses. What a simple idea, and with the property boom of the eighties you were laughing. I bet when you set out you never thought you would've ended up with your own building company. I enjoyed having you living round the corner for a few years, and I know that we never talked a lot, but at least we never fell out again. Mind you, David and Catherine... press it, Joe, quick, and again... Joe, its not working, press again.... Slowly, take it easy, slowly. That was bad, it came so quickly.

What? Oh yes, David and Catherine, they made up for the talking. What lovely grandchildren. They used to talk their heads off every time they came round, and I sat and listened and loved it. Many times I wished that your mum could have been sitting with us, joining in the chatter. She would have loved it as well. That she was missing out always upset me at first, but then I came to accept that my time with my grandchildren was a present from her, because if she hadn't died when she did then you probably wouldn't have come home, maybe never have met Emma, and I may never have had those times talking with my grandchildren. That may sound naive, but for me it helped me to accept something I couldn't alter. Perhaps talking with your children somehow helped to make up for all the times me and you never talked. Until tonight, of course.

Oh no! Again, press, Joe, press, press! Again Joe, it's not working, again!

"He's not relaxing. He's choking. What should I do?"
Rose was crying, and holding his free hand.
"Emma, what should I do?"
"Press it again, Joe, give him more of the injection, yeh 'ave to."
I pressed and pressed, and with each press the shudders in his

185

chest subsided ever so slightly, as though all the tension and anxiety were disappearing. But they weren't disappearing, they were
being transferred to me. With each press I gave more of the liquid
that would help him to die, and my heart was breaking as I did it.

"Oh Dad, don't die, don't die! There's so many things I want to
tell you. Don't die yet."

"Joe, his throat's filling with fluid. Oh, Joe, do something for
him."

"Rose, he's doing everything he can."

Michael pulled Rose close to him as she sobbed.

That's right, you look after her, Michael, look after my little girl.

When the fluid came I knew that his lung had collapsed, and I
put the curved pipe into his mouth and flicked the switch on the
machine by the bed, just like the nurse had said to do when this
happened. It drained the fluid from the back of his throat, then I
pressed the red button and kept it down until the syringe was
empty. I could hold back the tears no longer.

*Thanks Joe, I'll never forget tonight. But there's still time, you
know. What do you think?*

"Shall we race 'ome?"

"Okay, Dad."

"Right, this time we'll run all the way."

"All the way?"

"All the way. Can ye make it?"

"Watch me."

"Do ye want to be Romulus or Remus?"

"Romulus."

"Ready?"

"Ready."

"Go!"

*I set off fast, and I looked across the road to the pavement on the
other side, and could see Joe running as fast as his ten-year-old legs
could take him.*

"Go, Joe, go."

"Don't 'old back, Dad. I want to win properly or not at all."

"I won't."

I led to Churchill Parkway, and was still just ahead at Dene Drive. But the rise in the road as we neared the end of Queensway hit my legs and Joe was catching.

"I'm nearly with you, Dad."

By the lamp post we were almost neck and neck. The path to the cottages was about fifty yards away.

"Don't give up, Dad, don't give up."

"I won't. Fair and square, like I promised."

My legs were fading, and with only a few yards to go Joe pulled level with me and we reached the path together.

"Draw! It was a draw. I did it! I caught you. We got there together, Dad, didn't we!"

Then my dad sat up, the curved pipe fell from his mouth, and his eyes opened for the first time all night. He looked at Rose for a moment, then turned to me. His eyes were clear and fresh. From me he looked down the bed to the far wall. No, not the wall, he was looking beyond the wall, as though he could see something as clearly as if it was in the room. I turned but I saw nothing. One last time he turned to look at me. His eyes told me he had to go, and I knew that the light reflected in his eyes had come for him.

His body lay back on the bed and my dad went into the light.

Léonie Press specialises in local history, Cheshire social history, autobiography and books about France, including:

MEMORIES OF A CHESHIRE CHILDHOOD – MEMORIAL EDITION
Lenna Bickerton (ISBN 1 901253 00 7) £4.99

DIESEL TAFF
From 'The Barracks' to Tripoli
Austin Hughes (ISBN 1 901253 14 7) £8.99

A NUN'S GRAVE
A novel set in the Vale Royal of England
Alan K Leicester (ISBN 1 901253 08 2) £7.99

NELLIE'S STORY
A Life of Service
Elizabeth Ellen Osborne (ISBN 1 901253 15 5) £5.99

THE WAY WE WERE
Omnibus edition incorporating Over My Shoulder and Another's War
Les Cooper (ISBN 1 901253 07 4) £7.99

A HOUSE WITH SPIRIT
A Dedication to Marbury Hall
Jackie Hamlett and Christine Hamlett (ISBN 1 901253 19 8) £8.99

ONLY FOOLS DRINK WATER
Forty Years of Fun in Charente-Maritime
GEOFFREY MORRIS (ISBN 1 901253 10 4) £8.99

A BULL BY THE BACK DOOR
How an English family find their own paradise in rural France
Anne Loader (ISBN 1 901253 06 6) £8.99

From Léonie Press, 13 Vale Rd, Hartford, Northwich, Cheshire CW8 1PL.
More details: www.leoniepress.co.uk